Someone had [...]

Her car was strewn with flowers—black, dead roses. Deanna's first impulse was to flee, but the shadowy parking lot was too threatening. She jerked open the door of her car and lunged into the driver's seat.

She fought a rising sense of panic as she started the car and grasped the steering wheel with white-knuckled hands. As she drove, dead flowers jumped from the hood of the car and rushed past the windows like devilish spirits trying to get in.

Black roses caught in the wipers against the windshield. Hatred stabbed at her with every thorny stem, and the sensation of being trapped under the horrible bouquet choked her.

She wanted to stop and throw off every dead blossom... and she desperately wanted to know the identity of her valentine.

ABOUT THE AUTHOR

A multipublished author, Leona Karr pursued a career as a reading specialist until her first suspense book was published in 1980. She lives with her husband near Boulder, Colorado, and the Rocky Mountains—the setting for *Cupid's Dagger*. Mystery and romantic suspense are her favorite genres. When she isn't reading and writing, she happily spends her time spoiling a gaggle of giggling granddaughters.

Books by Leona Karr

HARLEQUIN INTRIGUE
120—TREASURE HUNT
144—FALCON'S CRY
184—HIDDEN SECRET
227—FLASHPOINT

Cupid's Dagger

Leona Karr

Harlequin Books

TORONTO • NEW YORK • LONDON
AMSTERDAM • PARIS • SYDNEY • HAMBURG
STOCKHOLM • ATHENS • TOKYO • MILAN
MADRID • WARSAW • BUDAPEST • AUCKLAND

To a dear friend, Jasmine Cresswell, who is special in many, many ways

ISBN 0-373-22262-9

CUPID'S DAGGER

Copyright © 1994 by Leona Karr.

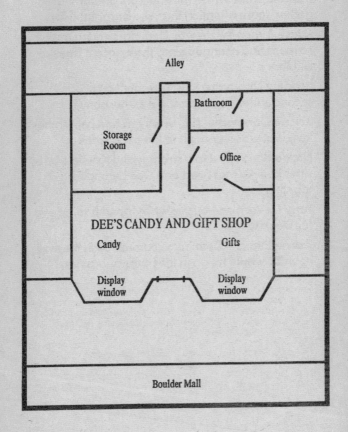

Alley

Bathroom

Storage
Room

Office

DEE'S CANDY AND GIFT SHOP

Candy

Gifts

Display
window

Display
window

Boulder Mall

CAST OF CHARACTERS

Deanna Donovan—This shop proprietor was getting more attention than she bargained for.

Reece Ryndell—He was Deanna's young love, but so much had changed since the innocent days of childhood.

Bradley Donovan—Just how bent on a reconciliation was Deanna's ex-husband?

Krissie Donovan—This baby girl had her mother's love, but was it enough to keep her safe?

Nickie Kendall—How strongly did Krissie's baby-sitter believe that Brad and Dee belonged together?

Tony DeVargas—Nickie's boyfriend had an eye for Deanna.

Darrel Evans—Deanna's competition in the mall, how far would he go in the name of business?

Chapter One

It was late, almost midnight. Brick paths winding through the three-block outdoor mall were empty, the stores closed. Leafless tree branches rose above snow-covered flower beds and made a spidery tracery against the night sky. He hunched down in his dark jacket and waited in the shadow of an old-fashioned popcorn wagon. His intense gaze was fixed on the windows of Dee's Candy and Gift Shop where a pretty brunette was putting in a Valentine display. She worked with quick, purposeful movements as if anxious to be finished.

Icy winds slipped down the slopes of the nearby Rocky Mountains, chilling the air and creating white puffs in front of his lips as he breathed. But he ignored the plunging temperature as a burning heat radiated through his body and a sense of power beaded hot sweat on his forehead. He smiled in satisfaction. She thought she'd put him out of her life forever but he had set in motion events to change all that. Everything was going according to plan. On the fourteenth of February, she'd be his sweetheart for always—his very own *dead* sweetheart. A satisfied laugh rumbled in his throat as he hugged himself. He'd taken too many risks already but that couldn't be helped. Murder had been the only expedient way to get her to come back to Boulder. Back to her childhood home.

Back to him.

DEANNA DONOVAN finished placing candy kisses around a large stuffed bear holding a heart-shaped box of chocolates. Dee's Candy and Gift Shop had been a tradition on the Pearl Street Mall since her parents had opened it when she was five years old. They had even named it for her. As she arranged lacy valentines upon a red velvet background, a deep sadness took all the joy from her creative efforts.

"You know that you and Krissie will always have a home with us," her parents had told Deanna when her divorce had become final last fall. She'd come home for Christmas, helped out in the store and enjoyed their traditional family holiday activities. When she returned to her sales job in Omaha, Nebraska, she planned to put things in order so she could move back home. She wanted to raise Krissie close to her daughter's grandparents. Two days later she received a call. Her parents had been shot during a holdup in the store. The horror of their death plunged Deanna into a nightmare.

She bit her lower lip as she threw away scraps of red paper and bits of white lace trimmings. Loneliness filled her with such pain that she wanted to walk out the door and never come back. But I have Krissie to think about, she told herself. Nothing was more important than her three-year-old daughter. Deanna felt that living in the old family home and town where she herself had grown up would provide the most stable environment for her little girl. She sighed. Heaven knows, there hadn't been much stability the first three years of Krissie's life.

I have to do my best to make a success of the store, she thought as she finished the window display. It was already February the first. In the next thirteen days, she'd have to move a lot of merchandise to show a profit.

The night wind quickened as she locked the front door of the store. For a moment she stood outside surveying the Valentine's Day decorations in the window. Red roses, chocolate hearts, chubby cupids shooting arrows, and candies printed with the messages, "I Love You" and "Be Mine." The traditional symbols of love were a mockery to the emptiness she felt inside. She'd be glad when Valentine's Day was over.

Clutching the collar of her long wool coat with a gloved hand, she bent her head forward against the surge of cold air. Parking at the mall was nearly impossible and the public garage was two blocks away. As her home was only four blocks north of the mall, it was easiest to walk to and from the store. Only she'd never been this late before. Since the murders of her parents, she always avoided being out alone at night. It was just common sense to take as many precautions as she could. Tonight couldn't be helped, though. She'd had to put in the extra hours in order to get the Valentine's Day display in the window.

Street lamps were clouded in a misty haze, and nightlights in the stores failed to penetrate shadows commanding doorways and alleys. As she passed an old-fashioned popcorn wagon, she thought she heard a faint sound. She darted a quick glance over her shoulder and quickened her steps, suddenly feeling she wasn't alone.

The mall was patrolled by foot policemen, but the night her parents had been robbed and killed, the horrible tragedy had gone unnoticed until two o'clock in the morning. Like most college towns, Boulder had a drug problem, and the police had told her that there had been a rash of burglaries all over town. She had been informed that the investigation of her parents' deaths was ongoing but so far there had been no new developments.

Her boots crunched on the icy walkway, sounding loudly in her ears. She left the mall and hurried up a side street lined with a spattering of small businesses. A flicker of a shadow in one of the windows mingled with her own as she hurried by. A feeling lingered that she wasn't alone. At the next corner, she stopped under the street lamp and looked back.

The sidewalk was empty.

A car's headlights came into view and caught her in their beam. An old blue Chevy slowed down and then stopped beside her. The passenger's window rolled down. "It's too cold to walk, Foxy. Get in," the man in the driver's seat ordered. "I'll give you a lift."

She couldn't see his face. Fearful that he might try to drag her into his car, she hurried down the sidewalk with her head facing forward and her hands in her pockets. She gave in to a rise of panic when the car kept pace with her brisk steps. The stalking Chevy was so close to the curb that she feared it would jump up on the sidewalk at any second and hit her. Deanna began to run.

Her breath was coming in short gasps and her chest burned when she reached the two-story house her parents had bought thirty years ago. Built of red brick, it was set back from the street, with a wide porch circling the front and sides. A reassuring light shone from the living-room window. Deanna dashed up the front steps, her only thought being to get safely inside.

A man's mocking voice floated after her. "Nice old house. See you soon, Foxy."

As the car drove away, she realized she'd led him right to her door. But she'd been too frightened to think ahead. Besides, what choice did she have? There wasn't any other place close where she could have gone.

As she turned her house key in the lock and gave the doorknob a turn, she realized that the door had been unlocked. Anger flared. She'd repeatedly warned Nicki, the college student who lived with her, to keep the door locked when she and Krissie were alone in the house. Anyone could walk in on them, fumed Deanna as she shut the door and turned the deadbolt. Nicki was blasé about everything, and was always chiding Deanna for being such a worrywart. But she hadn't had two parents shot in cold blood, Deanna thought defensively as she hung up her coat.

"Hi, is that you, Deanna?" asked Nicki's cheery voice from the living room.

"And what if it wasn't?" Deanna challenged as she came into the room.

Nicki was curled up on one end of the couch with a textbook resting in her lap and her fingers twisting a strand of her long blond hair in a habitual absent-minded manner. A frown crossed her pretty face as she saw Deanna's glower. "What's wrong?"

"The door was unlocked."

"Gee, Tony came by earlier. I guess I forgot to lock it after he left. Sorry. I have to hit the books. A test in biology tomorrow." She groaned as she looked at her watch. "Blast it all, it's nearly one and I've got three chapters left to read."

"Why do you always leave everything to the last minute?" Deanna snapped, knowing that she was unfairly transferring her anger about the unlocked door to Nicki's deplorable study habits.

"I don't know." The girl gave Deanna a sheepish smile. "I always find something better to do."

Deanna shifted her focus. "Did Krissie wake up at all?"

"Nope. The little angel's been asleep ever since you put her down."

"Have you looked in on her?" Krissie was asthmatic and especially prone to attacks at night. Sometimes her little chest labored for air and a frightening wheezing sound came from her lungs.

"Sure, I checked on her—a couple of times." Nicki's tone was slightly pained.

Stop it, Deanna told herself. *Quit nagging.* Nicki was wonderful with Krissie. She was lucky to have such a pleasant college student living with her. Even though Krissie went to day-care, the little girl needed a baby-sitter in the late afternoon and at times like tonight when Deanna had to work. Nicki had morning classes three days a week, and Deanna paid her to be home every afternoon at four o'clock to watch Krissie. Nicki might let other things slide, but she never neglected Krissie. Deanna felt guilty for having been so sharp with her.

Nicki eyed Deanna. "Your face is flushed. Did you run home?"

"Yes. Some creep was following me in his car. I wasn't thinking or I wouldn't have led him right to our doorstep. Anyway, if you see a blue Chevy cruising around, call the police. And you must re-

member to keep the door locked, Nicki. Don't open
it to anyone you don't know."

"Okay," Nicki said as if it didn't matter to her one
way or the other. She obviously thought Deanna was
being unduly paranoid.

"There are too many kooks running around,"
Deanna insisted. "And I worry that something could
happen to you and Krissie while I'm gone."

"Oh, don't worry, Tony keeps his eye on us."

Deanna choked back a retort. She didn't like Tony
DeVargas, and she wished that Nicki hadn't taken up
with him. He was conceited, arrogant and had wandering eyes. Deanna had seen him visually strip off
her clothes and leer at her with an infuriating smirk
on his tanned face. She avoided him whenever she
could.

After saying good-night to Nicki, Deanna hurried
upstairs. Deanna had given Krissie her old bedroom, and had taken the one next to it for herself.
She'd rented the one at the back of the house to
Nicki, and planned to turn her parents' large front
bedroom into her own private sitting room. That
would leave the downstairs living room free for Nicki
to entertain her boyfriends, which at the moment
seemed to be exclusively Tony DeVargas.

Standing next to her daughter's bed, Deanna
looked down at her sleeping child. Krissie lay with
soft brown hair curling around her face and a fringe
of long eyelashes shadowing her cheeks. She was
small for her age, and fragile. Deanna resisted the

urge to take her in her arms and hug her. She tucked in the covers gently, then bent over and kissed her daughter's warm cheek. She left the door open to the hall so she could hear the child if she called.

In her bedroom, Deanna changed to a warm brushed wool gown and was just slipping into bed when she heard Nicki come upstairs to her room. She hoped the girl had remembered to turn off the living-room lights. Keeping the utility bill down was going to be a problem.

A bone-deep weariness overtook her as she slipped into bed. Tomorrow she would have to check the store's inventory and decide what she should reorder. The shop offered specialty items in addition to a wide assortment of candies. She wished she'd paid more attention to the business part of the store while her parents were alive. Then, after she was married, Brad hadn't wanted her to work, an insult to his male ego, of course. She'd been lucky to find a clerking job in a small dress shop after the divorce. The degrees she'd taken in art and psychology hadn't prepared her to enter the work force.

She'd married Bradley Donovan when they were seniors at Colorado University. He had been a BMC—big man on campus, she mused wryly. An outstanding quarterback, he'd been chosen as most valuable player and they had celebrated by getting married the day after graduation.

Deanna sighed. Brad had tried professional football and failed. He'd accepted assistant coaching jobs with small college teams, but his ego always got in the way and his contracts were never renewed. The last fiasco involved a campus scandal with a cheerleader. Deanna had filed for divorce. The proceedings had been ugly.

But that was over now. She should get some sleep. Tomorrow would be soon enough to face all the challenges that awaited her.

She had just turned off her bedroom lamp when the doorbell rang. Her heart was suddenly racing. *Bad news came at night.*

She sat up, shoved her feet into her slippers and knotted the belt of her robe as she hurried down the hall. When she reached the top of the stairs, she felt a rush of cold air sweeping up the staircase.

A small light in the hall below played upon the narrow windows overlooking the front porch. Deanna was halfway down the stairs when she let out a frightened cry.

The heavy front door was wide open!

She froze on the bottom step and screamed.

A butcher knife pinned a large red valentine heart to the door. Something crimson dripped from the blade.

Chapter Two

Nicki came rushing down the stairs, clad in a skimpy nightshirt that barely covered her rounded derriere. "What's the matter?"

Deanna couldn't speak. She just pointed.

Nicki pushed by Deanna and walked over to the door. She studied the mutilated red heart and dripping knife for a long moment and then sniffed. "Ketchup." When she turned around, there was a grin on her face. "It's okay, Deanna. It's just Tony. He's always playing practical jokes. What a nut."

"Tony?" Deanna echoed. "He did this?"

She giggled. "He was teasing me tonight about stabbing him in the heart when I shooed him out early."

"But the door. I locked the door. How did he get it open?"

Nicki thought for a moment, then she eyed her shoulder bag, which she habitually left hanging over the newel post at the bottom of the stairs. "I'll bet he was planning to play a joke on me and took my keys on the way out tonight.'' Nicki opened her purse. Her keys were lying on top. ''He must have slipped them back in after he opened the door.''

A joke. That's all it was, Deanna told herself as she took a deep breath. ''Well, you tell Mr. Tony DeVargas in no uncertain terms that I don't appreciate his sense of humor. And if he ever does something like this again, he'll be in more trouble than he bargained for. Now, please get that thing off the door and—''

She broke off as Krissie's little voice came from upstairs. ''Mommy...Mommy.''

''Don't worry, Deanna. I'll set him straight,'' Nicki called as Deanna hurried upstairs.

''It's all right,'' Deanna said soothingly as she gathered the little girl into her arms. She kissed the top of the child's warm head. ''Go back to sleep.''

Deanna was furious with Tony and his macabre sense of humor. She mentally rehearsed a few scalding words to lay on him the next time he came to the house.

''You stay with me,'' Krissie begged.

''All right, honey. But only for a little while.'' She didn't want to start a habit that she would have to break sooner or later.

Deanna took off her robe and slipped under the covers beside Krissie in the narrow bed that once had been hers. She cushioned her daughter's head against her shoulder and soon Krissie's breathing told her that the child had fallen asleep.

Because this had been her bedroom for so many years, Deanna felt more at home at that moment than at any time since she'd been back. Gentle memories of laughter, tears and dreams flowed over her as she lay there, cradling her daughter. She wanted to give Krissie the same kind of happy childhood she'd known in this very room. She vowed to be the best single parent any child could have. Deanna lay there for a long time, then reluctantly went back to her own room and climbed into her cold, empty bed.

A guarded uneasiness kept her body tense and rigid as she lay there staring at the ceiling. She'd always felt competent and secure in the knowledge that she could take care of herself, but her parents' deaths threatened to weaken that confidence.

It was foolish to let a stupid prank upset her so, she lectured herself. She'd always prided herself on having steady nerves and the ability to face problems straight-on. But the changes in her life had come too fast, she reasoned, her divorce less than a year ago, the stress of finding and keeping a job, and then the loss of her parents. Now she was back in the town where she'd grown up, and she was facing new challenges. All these things had combined to set her life reeling like an off-balance top.

She listened to the creaking sounds of the old house, the brush of leafless branches against the window and the quiet popping of settling boards. Familiar sounds and strange ones, too. She thought she heard a scraping on the side porch below her windows, but the sound was lost as a whine of air caught the eaves of the house.

Relax, she told herself. *It's nothing but the wind.*

HE CURSED the aluminum lawn chair that he'd accidentally knocked over as he made his way around the porch to the front of the house. The chair didn't belong there. He knew every inch of the old-fashioned porch that skirted the front and sides of the house. Summer furniture had always been placed to the right of the front door, not along the sides. He felt betrayed by the change, as if she were trying to trick him. He carried the chair around to the front and set it where it belonged. There, that was better. He wanted everything as it had been before. The only thing that would be different was the way she treated him.

She'd been frightened. He knew that. Her shrill cry had shown that she was shocked. Even though he hadn't been close enough to hear what she was saying, he was satisfied that his first valentine had sent the right message.

He slipped down the side steps. In the shadow of the barren willow tree, he stopped and glanced up at her bedroom window. He remembered the white furniture and pretty pink quilt in her narrow bed from when she was in grade school. Then in high school, she'd hung new wallpaper and pictures and added posters of Elvis. Had she changed the room since she'd been back?

He smiled as his fingers closed over the key in his pocket. He'd have to take a look. Even if she installed new locks, he could get inside easily enough.

DEANNA WAS LATE opening the store the next morning. At breakfast, Krissie had spilled milk all over herself and needed to be changed. Nicki couldn't help because she'd overslept and didn't have time for anything but a piece of toast and a dash out the door. The little van that picked up students for the Mother Goose Day-care had to wait five minutes while Deanna got Krissie into dry clothes.

Deanna waved goodbye to her daughter and walked from the curb to the house. As she climbed the front steps, she noticed the lawn chair sitting to the left of the door. Krissie must have dragged it around from the side porch, she thought idly as she went inside and shut the door.

She quickly put the kitchen to rights, resisting the temptation to have another cup of coffee. A luxury you can't afford, she told herself as she took a hot shower and dressed in a purple sweater and pants. She tied a paisley scarf around her neck and added tiny pearl earrings. The flattering outfit should have brightened her mood, but as she brushed her curly brunette hair, violet shadows under her eyes seemed to deepen. She made a grimace at herself that was funny enough to ease her lips into a faint smile.

She groaned when she looked at her watch. Hurriedly, she raced down the stairs and grabbed a ski jacket and knitted scarf from the coat closet. As she locked the front door, her eyes fastened on the deep cut in the oak panel. *A knife in your heart.* Deanna couldn't suppress the shiver that crept up her spine.

The brisk walk to the store cleared away her depression, the exercise leaving her invigorated and ready to face the day. A delivery truck marked United Federal was in the unloading zone behind the store when she arrived, the driver leaning against his vehicle.

"Sorry to have kept you waiting," she apologized as she unlocked the back door.

More boxes of candy. Her parents must have ordered them right after Christmas, she thought as she looked at the invoice and groaned. She'd have to get busy and do some promotion to move it between now and Valentine's Day.

Nellie Shaw, the middle-aged saleswoman who had worked for her parents for years, came to work at noon. Until then, Deanna would handle customers and take care of routine office tasks, which included making out the bank deposit—her mother's daily job.

Deanna bit her lip. Her parents had never kept the day's receipts longer than overnight. Why hadn't the thief been satisfied with just taking the money? Why had he forced her parents into the small storage room and then shot them? The horror of it poured over her again. Maybe her father had put up a fight, Deanna speculated. He'd always been protective of his "womenfolk" as he called her and her mother. Some of his stubbornness had been passed on to Deanna. She clenched her fists. She knew that she'd probably lose her head if anyone tried to harm Krissie.

The chime over the front door sounded and Deanna reined in her emotions. She put a smile on her face and sold two pounds of chocolate-pecan clusters to Mrs. Collins, a gray-haired lady who expressed her deepest sympathy for Deanna's loss.

"Such nice people, your parents," Mrs. Collins sighed. "After your visit last Christmas, your folks said you might be coming back to Boulder. They were hoping that you and Krissie would make your home with them again. I know they'd be gratified to know you're not selling the store."

"I won't unless I have to." Deanna handed her the box of candy.

"And you can be sure that all of us will continue to be good customers here at Dee's Candy and Gift Shop."

"Thank you. I appreciate it," Deanna replied sincerely.

"I know that your folks were worried that the new Sweet Shoppe would cut into their business." Mrs. Collins pursed her lips. "Personally, I think it was a stab in the back for Darrel Evans to work for your parents and then go into competition with them by opening another candy and gift store in the same mall.''

Deanna gave Mrs. Collins a noncommittal smile. She wasn't going to add more grist for the rumor mill. She knew her father had been upset to lose Darrel, not so much because of the competitive business but because her parents had been doing a lot of traveling the last few years and had felt confident about leaving the store in Darrel's hands. More and more, he had functioned as an assistant manager.

I could surely use his help now, thought Deanna as a new wave of desolation swept over her. She'd be glad when Nellie Shaw arrived. I'm really not up to waiting on customers, she thought as Mrs. Collins left the store.

Another United Federal delivery truck pulled up at the back door. A driver brought in one box marked "Fragile," shipped from Southwest Pottery Company in New Mexico.

More inventory?

"Just put it here," she said, moving aside the unopened boxes that had been delivered earlier.

"Got three more for you."

Deanna tried to keep the dismay from her expression as she signed his clipboard. She had no idea what plans her parents had for marketing the Indian pottery. The store had never offered such specialized crafts. Maybe her mother and father had planned to change the emphasis of the store, she reasoned. Less candy, more artistic giftware? The only thing she was certain about was that she'd have to turn over this new stock quickly in order to keep up the cash flow.

By the time Nellie arrived at noon, Deanna had the bank deposit ready and was glad to leave the store in the saleslady's capable hands, even though those same hands were forever sampling chocolates displayed in the glass bins. Two mints disappeared into the portly woman's mouth as Deanna put on her jacket.

"I'll be back in a few minutes," Deanna told her.

Nellie studied Deanna openly. "You look a mite peaked, if you ask me. Why don't you go someplace and have yourself a nice lunch? No need for you to be here every minute. I can handle things."

"Thanks, Nellie. Maybe I'll grab a sandwich. Things were so hectic this morning I forgot to fix a lunch."

The temperature on the bank's outside monitor read forty-eight degrees. A real heat wave, she thought wryly as she pushed into the bank's lobby and took her place in line.

She had been standing there a couple of minutes when the back of her neck began to prickle. She turned around. Only one person stood behind her in the line, an elderly man clutching his social security check. Deanna gave him a vague smile and then let her eyes sweep around the lobby. She didn't see anyone she knew. No one was looking at her. She

shrugged off the feeling that she was being ob-
served.

When she came out of the bank, she decided that
she'd take Nellie's advice and stop somewhere for a
sandwich. She chose the College Kitchen, an infor-
mal restaurant that offered soups and sandwiches.
She was surprised to find that Darrel Evans's new
store was located next door to the café.

A good location, Deanna thought begrudgingly as
she stood outside the shop. The Sweet Shoppe's windows were filled with all kinds of chocolate special-
ties: baskets filled with dipped strawberries; long-
stemmed chocolate roses; mints wrapped in embossed gold paper; lovely candy dishes of every fan-
ciful color and design.

"Well, what do you think?" Darrel Evans's round
face was creased with a broad smile as she turned
around. Somewhere in his early forties, the man
bounced when he walked, used his hands for talking
and gave the impression of possessing unlimited energy. He stood so close to her that she could feel his
warm breath on her face.

"Very nice, Darrel," she said, stepping back
slightly. "Congratulations."

"Thanks. I have to thank your folks for teaching
me everything I know." A dark expression crossed
his face. "I'm sorry about what happened. I told
your dad he should have some kind of weapon, with
all the robberies going on, but he wouldn't listen. I
was always afraid when I worked late in the store."

"He didn't believe in guns."

"Well, I do," he said with spirit. "Nobody's going to catch me off guard."

"How long have you been open?"

"Since Thanksgiving."

She didn't know very much about Darrel. He'd been hired after her marriage and she'd only briefly visited with him on her trips home.

"How's your mother?" she asked in the awkward pause.

"She passed on.... Cancer." Deanna began to speak, but Darrel rushed on. "Sure miss her. Bless her, she left me enough money to buy this store. And there's no need for us to be unfriendly competitors, is there? There's enough business for both of us. Maybe we can help each other," he suggested brightly.

"Of course," Deanna reassured him, knowing that the advantage would be all hers. He knew a heck of a lot more about running a business than she did.

"Well, see you around." With a wave, he bounced into his store, reminding her of Tigger in Krissie's *Winnie the Pooh* book.

Suppressing a smile, she went next door to the College Kitchen. The café was crowded and the only empty table was a small one at the back. Her waitress was a college student, quick and efficient, and Deanna was enjoying a large bowl of clam chowder when a shadow crossed her table.

"May I join you?"

Deanna glanced up at the man and shook her head. "I'm sorry, but I prefer to eat alone."

He didn't move. He just stood there, his hands shoved down in the pockets of his ski jacket.

"I'm not looking for company," she told him crisply.

"Are you sure?" he asked with a smile teasing the corners of his lips.

She put down her spoon. "Please leave or I'll call the manager."

"You don't remember me, Dee Dee," he said sadly.

The use of the childhood nickname startled her. She stared at him. Dark hair drifted forward around a finely sculptured face. His eyes were a strange shade of gray feathered with blue. The unusual color stirred recognition. Could it be?

"Reece?"

"The same."

She couldn't believe it. He had been the oldest boy in the neighborhood crowd when she was growing up. At least four years older than most of the other kids on the block, Reece Ryndell had been an acceptable chaperon, keeping them from getting into trouble with their parents when they were younger, and handing out words of wisdom when they were older. He had left Boulder just about the time her life had begun to revolve exclusively around Brad.

She sprang to her feet and hugged him. "I didn't recognize you." She searched his lean face. "Oh, please sit down. I feel so dumb, Reece. I should have recognized you.''

She had completely lost track of this friend who had been the object of an adolescent crush when she was sixteen. Of course, she'd kept her romantic fantasies to herself, knowing that as kind as he was, a man of twenty wouldn't be anything but embarrassed about her attentions. She thought about him a lot but had never known where he had settled.

"Don't apologize. As my mother keeps telling me, I'm just a shadow of my former self." He put a couple of books down on the table and took a chair opposite her. He smiled at her puzzled expression. "It's all right. You can ask me."

"You've been ill?"

He nodded. "But it's nothing dire. In a couple of months I should be back to normal."

"What happened?"

"I went overseas to work as an engineer for a big oil company. My contract was about up when I was hospitalized with one of those obscure foreign diseases. I finally made it home."

"I'm sorry. I didn't know." She cursed herself for not asking about him when she had been home last Christmas. His parents not only lived in a house a few blocks away from hers, but Mr. Ryndell, a widower, owned the bookstore in the mall that specialized in mystery books. The Dark Corner Bookstore was a popular haunt for readers of whodunits. "How long have you been back?"

He hesitated and the way he said, "Just a few weeks," made her wonder whether he was lying.

The waitress took his order and they chatted a few minutes about the old neighborhood.

"Most of the houses have changed owners, I guess," he said.

She nodded. There had been no sense of homecoming for her. All her old friends were gone. Only one neighbor, Mrs. Caruthers, had dropped by when Krissie was at the day-care center and Deanna had found it hard to talk about the good old days. Her daughter, Ellen, who had been Deanna's best friend all through school, had married and moved away.

"I hear you divorced Brad." Reece bit into the sandwich the waitress had brought.

"That's right," she said, wondering what his marital status was. A quiver of feminine interest in him caught her by surprise. "How about you? Are you still single and uncommitted?"

"All of the above."

"You always did love 'em and leave 'em," she teased.

His gray-blue eyes searched her face. His sensitive mouth softened. "I'm sorry marriage didn't work out for you. But I can't say that I'm surprised."

She flared at his honesty and then remembered that frankness was the one thing you could always depend on from Reece Ryndell. He never minced words. "All of us have twenty-twenty vision after the fact," she said evenly.

"So you've come home to stay?"

"If I can keep the business going. I've settled in my parents' house with my little girl and rented out a room to a college student."

"I know. News travels in the old neighborhood just as fast as it used to. I thought I'd drop in on you sometime but didn't want to hurry it."

"What about you? Will you be staying in Boulder long?"

"That depends ... on a lot of things. At the moment I'm helping my dad out in the bookstore. Great place to hide from the world and bone up on such things as poisons, knives and guns."

She gasped.

"I'm sorry," he said quickly. "Have the police come up with anything on your parents' deaths?"

She shook her head. "I guess there wasn't much to go on."

"I understand that there wasn't any sign of a break-in. I mean, the newspaper said the coroner put the time of death after nine o'clock, so the store would have been locked up by then. They must have let the robber in ... or he was in the store when it closed."

Her lower lip trembled.

"I shouldn't have brought up the subject. Sorry. I guess being raised around mystery books has left its mark on me. Can't help speculating about these things."

"It's all right. I just still can't believe it happened. Not to my mother and dad." She took a deep breath. "The police said they've had a rash of robberies lately. Boulder isn't the quiet little town it was when we were growing up." A shadow passed over her face.

He reached out and touched her hand. "Don't forget I'm around in case you're interested."

"Of course, I'm interested."

"Are you sure?"

What was he asking? She certainly wasn't ready for any romantic involvements, but an old friend would help fill the void in her life. "I'd like it if you dropped by the house sometime. We're still neighbors, you know."

His gray eyes locked with hers. "It's too bad it took you such a hell of a long time to grow up, Dee Dee." He stood, picked up both checks and walked away before she could answer.

While he was still at the cash register, she noticed he had left his books at the table. She picked them up and her eyes froze on the title of the top one.

The Bleeding Heart Murder.

Chapter Three

Reece's lean face was creased in a frown as he entered the bookstore and gave an absentminded wave to a pretty cashier who looked at him with a wistful smile. He had made a private retreat for himself on the second floor by moving an old scarred desk and chair close to a narrow window at the rear of the long building. Hidden by a bank of bookshelves and boxes, he spent his time cataloging, pricing, or reading books of his choice. Sometimes he just sat there.

After his encounter with Deanna, he leaned back in the old chair and stared out the window. Dark shadows deepened the smoky gray of his eyes, and his jaw was set in a rigid line.

He hadn't been ready to meet her face-to-face. Stupid, he swore to himself. And dangerous. When he had seen her sitting alone at the table, he hadn't been able to resist making contact with her. The fact that she hadn't even recognized him reinforced the jealous anger he had felt when she'd filled her life with Bradley Donovan. Until the puffed-up football hero had come along, they'd enjoyed a special relationship. Sure, Reece had been older and had been a kind of brotherly protector through her teens, but as she had matured, his feelings for her had deepened. Hell, admit it, an inner voice mocked, you wanted to carry her off to your den like some damned Lochinvar.

His mouth tightened. It was true. All his protective, possessive feelings had exploded into a frustrated passion that nearly drove him crazy. And before he'd had a chance to express them, she'd gotten herself married to Bradley Donovan. But she was home again and so was he, he thought as a quiver of anticipation sluiced through him.

He hadn't been completely honest with her about his physical and mental condition. He'd been to hell and back. And being on the edge of death in a foreign country had taught him one thing: *Take what you want from life before it's too late.*

DEANNA RETURNED to the store and spent the afternoon putting up more valentine displays and working on some publicity ads for the local paper. As she labored over accounts payable, she told herself that increased business would pay for the added expenses.

All afternoon, her thoughts strayed to Reece. What a surprise to see him again. Memories came flooding back. He'd always been a strong support in her life. She couldn't count the times he'd offered her a comforting shoulder for some childish disappointment. She wondered if he'd been aware of the crush she'd had on him when she was in high school. Dates with boys her own age had lacked the excitement she felt when Reece was around. How proud she'd been to be with this tall, handsome "older" man when he bought her a soda or dropped by the house with a book she might like to read. Much to her chagrin, he'd always treated her as his kid sister.

When she was a freshman in college, he was already in graduate school and their old easy companionship disappeared. Deanna's forehead furrowed as she tried to remember the last time that Reece had come over to the house and sat on the front porch with her. It must have been about the time she met Brad. Sadly enough, she'd been too busy with her flamboyant football hero to even miss Reece's presence.

Their reunion in the café had left her with conflicting emotions. His sensitive smile was still devastating, but his face showed the ravages of a serious illness. The more she thought about it, the more she realized there was something about him that made her uneasy. His choice of reading material for one thing. And the way he'd brought up the subject of her parents' murders.

She wasn't certain that the Dark Corner Bookstore was a healthy place for him to be. Though he was a stranger to her now, it was apparent that the changes in Reece Ryndell might go deeper than just his appearance.

At five o'clock, she locked up the store. Nellie was surprised at the early closing because Deanna's folks had stayed open till six o'clock and had had extended hours until nine o'clock on special occasions.

"I can't ever remember closing up at five," the older woman protested. The idea of losing hourly wages obviously didn't appeal to her.

"I'm sorry," Deanna told her. "But I have to balance my working hours with taking care of my daughter."

"I could close up for you," Nellie offered.

Deanna shook her head. "I don't think that's a good idea. Not after what happened. The burglar waited until my parents were here alone. Maybe we can stay open later in the spring when it doesn't get dark so early."

Nellie left the store in a huff.

The streetlights had come on but most of the stores were still open. As Deanna hurried along the mall, she glanced in the store windows. When a white teddy bear with black ears, nose and paws caught her eye, she impulsively went into the store and bought it for Krissie.

She was glad she'd be home in time to fix a nice dinner and to play with Krissie before bedtime. With the teddy bear clutched in her arms, she bounded up the front steps of the house with a lightness in her step that hadn't been there all day.

Deanna was relieved that the front door was locked and that Nicki was following her instructions. As she opened the door, she paused for a moment and looked at the deep gash in the front panel. On some level of awareness, she felt an uncurling of fear. It disappeared as quickly as it had come and she dismissed it as an unwarranted reaction to a sick joke.

"I'm home," she called as she hung her coat in the closet.

When she entered the living room, Nicki was curled up in her usual position on the couch and Krissie sat in the middle of the floor making a red and yellow tower with a set of new building blocks. Her daughter's blue eyes shone brightly as she looked up at Deanna. "See what Daddy brought me."

Deanna's chest tightened. She sent Nicki a startled look. "Brad was here?"

Nicki unwound her legs and closed her book with a snap. "Yep. About three this afternoon. I didn't know what to do. I mean, I opened the door and there he was. Smiling and holding a package. Gee, I didn't know he was such a handsome hunk!" She gave Deanna a sheepish smile. "He charmed the heck out of me."

Deanna tried to keep her voice even. "Did he leave any message for me?"

Nicki twisted a strand of hair. "Not really. I mean, he asked how you were doing, and everything." She followed Deanna into the kitchen.

"How long did he stay?"

"About a half hour. And, Deanna, he was so sweet with Krissie. I could tell he's been missing her."

"Really." Deanna's tone was edged with sarcasm. "That's surprising since he hasn't phoned or tried to see her until now."

"He said he'd been busy, interviewing for some Colorado coaching jobs." *Damn!* Why couldn't her ex-husband lose himself somewhere in one of the other forty-nine states? Brad might make a different kind of woman a good husband, but he'd always suffocated her with his male superiority. She'd accumulated five years of emotional baggage living with him and that was enough. When they decided on divorce, he'd predicted that she'd never be able to care for herself and Krissie. She certainly didn't need him around, undermining her confidence at every turn. "I wonder how long he's been in town."

"He didn't say." Nicki gave Deanna a speculative look. "But I think he wants you two to get back together. I mean, he asked all about the store and how you were managing all by yourself. Acted real lonesome, if you know what I mean."

"Don't be taken in by that 'poor me' act of his," Deanna snapped. "Brad's a master of manipulation." The acidity of her words surprised her. She thought she'd laid all her resentment and bitterness to rest, but Brad's unexpected intrusion into her new life had revived her negative feelings.

"What do you want me to do if he comes around again?" Nicki sent her a teasing grin. "Stand in the door with a shotgun?"

Deanna took a deep breath. "Of course not. He has the right to visit Krissie, but I want him to make arrangements. I don't want him showing up here when I'm not home." Was Brad using their daughter to get back into her life? He had a lot of faults but she didn't think him guilty of that kind of subterfuge. "I want to be fair," she told Nicki, "but I just don't want him taking Krissie without my permission."

Nicki shrugged. "Okay, but he seems like a real nice guy. He talked a lot about how much he liked this house and about the good times. He was glad that you and Krissie had come back to Boulder to live." Nicki's voice softened. "His eyes got kinda misty. I sort of felt sorry for him."

Deanna bit back a caustic reply and turned away without answering. It had taken her five years to learn that Brad's ego needed constant nourishment.

Krissie wandered into the kitchen. "I'm hungry."

Deanna picked her up and snuggled her neck. "Help Mommy decide what to cook for supper."

"Why don't we order pizza?" Nicki suggested.

"I'll bet that's what you had for lunch," Deanna teased.

"Nope, I had a hamburger."

"Well, how about a nicely balanced meal, with vegetables and everything? It's called brain food."

Nicki laughed. "I could sure use some of that."

"How about you fixing a salad?" Deanna suggested as she put Krissie down and began chopping chicken and vegetables for a stir-fry dinner. Between the two of them, the meal was on the table in only a few minutes and even Krissie ate most of her helping instead of just moving the food around on her plate.

"I've got to finish a blasted research paper tonight," Nicki told Deanna as they ate. "I'll probably stay at the library until it closes."

"I don't like the idea of you hitchhiking up to the campus. Why don't you take my car?"

Nicki gave a dismissive wave of her hand. "I only accept rides from girls. Besides, Tony will probably bring me home."

Deanna bit her lip. Nicki was a paid baby-sitter and a boarder in her house, Deanna told herself, and not her responsibility. Still, she couldn't help worrying about the girl's safety. She had an uneasy feeling about Tony, and there were lots of nuts around, like the guy who had followed her home.

"Do you have your key?" she asked Nicki as she prepared to lock the door after her.

"Sure thing." She gave Deanna a reassuring smile. "See you later." She bounded down the front steps, her backpack bouncing on her shoulders.

In spite of the good dinner Krissie had eaten, she was fussy and querulous. Even before bedtime she had begun to cough. A dry, seal-like bark. There was a warning wheezing in her breathing. The bedtime routine seemed to take forever—two fairy tales, one glass of water and three trips to the bathroom before Krissie was finally settled in bed.

"This was my room when I was a little girl like you," Deanna said as she tucked her in. "And I was very, very happy here."

"Not our house. Daddy said."

Deanna's mouth went dry. "Of course, it's our house. Grandma and Grandpa left it to you and me."

"Daddy said no."

"Well, he was wrong. Now quit worrying," she said brightly. She kissed Krissie's forehead. "Here's your new teddy bear to keep you company," she said, putting the stuffed animal in Krissie's arms. "Now, you close your eyes and go to sleep."

The child hugged the toy fiercely as her little chest rose and fell in an agitated rhythm. The doctor had warned Deanna that stress could trigger an attack. *Damn Brad!* How dare he make the child feel insecure? Krissie had been free of problems since their arrival in Boulder—until Brad's visit.

As the minutes passed, Krissie's breathing grew worse.

Deanna had had a pediatrician check Krissie over when they'd moved here. He'd approved the medication she'd been taking that accelerated her heartbeat but opened her lungs for more oxygen. Deanna gave Krissie the prescribed dose and waited for Krissie's breathing to become less labored.

An hour later, Deanna knew that the medication wasn't going to work. Krissie's hollow gasps for air were frightening. Deanna called the doctor.

"Better take her to the hospital. I'll meet you there."

As quickly as Deanna could, she loaded Krissie into the car, blankets wrapped around her like a cocoon. She was thankful that Nicki had not taken her up on her offer of taking the car that night, but wished that her boarder had stayed home. Having someone with her would have been a great help. Not that Brad had ever been around during any emergencies. During Krissie's last attack, he'd been away for a football game.

Deanna pulled up to the emergency entrance. Immediately, two attendants whisked Krissie inside. An hour later, she was breathing normally with the help of an oxygen tube in her nose.

"Better leave her overnight," the doctor advised. He looked at his watch. "Eleven o'clock."

"I think I should stay with her," Deanna protested.

The fatherly physician touched her shoulder. "Go home. No need for you to sit up all night with her. Krissie will get a good night's sleep and be raring to go in the morning. You'll need your energy to keep up with her.''

"I'd rather stay here," Deanna said stubbornly.

"Who's going to take care of your little girl if you get sick?'' he asked in a reasonable tone.

With a quiver of her lower lip, she admitted, "There's only me.''

"Then you have to make sure that nothing happens to you and your health, Mrs. Donovan.''

He was right, of course. No use lying to herself. She had a business to run and a household to keep going. She'd need all her strength to stay on top of her responsibilities. Krissie would be looked after in the hospital. She was sleeping peacefully now.

"All right. But if she wakes up during the night and needs me, I want to be called." She kissed her sleeping daughter and whispered, "See you in the morning, darling.''

Deanna left the hospital by the front entrance and walked through the parking lot. With her hands stuck in her pockets, she bit her lip to control a wash of tears flowing into her eyes. She was worried, tired and filled with a sense of helplessness.

Later she tried to remember if there had been any kind of movement, any warning that someone lurked nearby, watching her walk between the narrow lines of cars. If there had been, her thoughts were too heavy to notice.

When she reached her car, she was jolted to attention. Like a funeral bier, her car was strewn with flowers—black, dead roses.

Someone had left her a hate bouquet.

Chapter Four

Deanna's first impulse was to flee to the lighted building, but the long shadowy parking lot with its legion of dark caverns between cars was too threatening. She jerked open the door of her car and lunged into the driver's seat. With trembling fingers she shoved the lock into place.

Black flowers were tucked into the wipers and scattered across the windshield. They obliterated her vision. Their ugliness smothered her in a sensation that suddenly became claustrophobic. She closed her eyes and struggled against a hysteria that threatened to immobilize her. The deliberately malevolent act appalled her. Hatred reeked from every dead blossom.

She had to get away before— Before what? Her mind refused to make any sense out of the ugliness. Was the hate bouquet a warning of some kind? Who would send such an ugly message to her? And why?

Still fighting a rising sense of panic, she started the car with trembling fingers and turned on the wipers. Their movement dislodged enough of the flowers to give her limited visibility. Shadows on the edge of her vision moved like leering faces pressed against a pane of glass. Her heart thumped wildly in her own ears as she backed the car out of its parking space and drove to the nearest exit. She grasped the steering wheel with white-knuckled hands as she headed east toward the police station on Thirty-third Street.

As she drove, dead flowers jumped from the hood of the car and rushed past the windows like devilish spirits trying to get in. The black roses caught in the wipers stood against the windshield as if mocking her. Hatred stabbed at her with every thorny stem, and the sensation of being trapped under the horrible bouquet remained. She desperately wanted to stop the car and throw off every dead blossom but she didn't. She was afraid of a nameless terror that waited for her.

She glanced repeatedly in the mirror. When a pair of headlights kept a measured distance behind her, new fear stabbed at her. She drove faster. *Don't panic,* she told herself over and over again. Anyone responsible for the hate bouquet wouldn't follow her into a police station. The pair of headlights stayed at a discreet distance—too far away for her to see what kind of car they belonged to. The beam wasn't dim. An old car? She'd forgotten about the old Chevy and the man who had called her Foxy, but now she wondered. Was he the one harassing her with dead roses?

With a sigh of relief, Deanna swung the car into a parking lot at the side of a modern building housing the police department. Before she got out, she looked back at the street. No sign of the car that had been behind her. It must have turned off on Thirty-second Street, she reasoned. *When her destination had become clear to the driver.*

The sturdy, middle-aged policeman who came out to look at her car and the few roses tucked under the wipers just shook his head. "These college kids come up with something different every day. Used to be toilet paper they spread all over everything just to harass someone. Or spray-paint graffiti. At least, you don't have a cleanup job with dead flowers," he said as he dislodged the remaining black roses. "How many cars did they get with their sick joke?"

"I . . . I don't know." Was it her car that had been targeted? Or, had other cars been involved? The tightness in her chest eased. "Do you think that's what it was? Just a college prank?"

"What else could it be?"

Yes, what else? Relief poured over her. She was embarrassed that she'd reported the incident. It must be her parents' deaths that were making her view everything with such suspicion. Her reaction to Tony's little joke had been the same—sudden fright and panic. What was happening to her? She'd never shown any inclination toward paranoia before.

In order to justify her actions, she told the policeman about the man who had followed her home the other night. "He almost ran up on the sidewalk."

"Did you get his license plate number?"

"No, I didn't," she said regretfully. "It was dark and I was intent on getting home as fast as I could."

"Well, unless you have some positive identification and proof of definite harassment, we can't do a thing." He shook his head. "If we locked up all the fellows who tried to pick up girls, we'd have half the student body behind bars."

His common-sense remarks made her feel more foolish than ever. She quickly thanked him for his time.

"You should avoid situations where you're vulnerable," he lectured. "A pretty young woman like yourself shouldn't be out alone at this time of night. It's almost midnight."

"Yes, I know." She choked back a defensive reply that she'd had little choice when she'd had to take her daughter to the hospital. Despite the policeman's reassurance, she was still fighting uneasiness as she drove home and into the garage at the rear of the property.

She had left the house so hurriedly with Krissie in her arms that she hadn't turned off any lights. Windows in the kitchen, living room and Krissie's bedroom glowed brightly. Nicki's room at the back remained dark and Deanna wondered if the young woman was home yet.

When Deanna realized she hadn't locked the back door after putting Krissie in the car, she was glad she'd left the house well lit.

"Nicki...Nicki," she called as she entered the kitchen from the small back porch.

Everything in the kitchen was just as Deanna had left it. No sign that Nicki had fixed her usual bedtime snack. She hadn't come home.

Deanna glanced at her watch. Twelve-fifteen. The library closed at ten. The girl probably went somewhere for pizza, Deanna thought, pushing aside a quiver of uneasiness.

Go to bed, she told herself. Krissie was sound asleep under the watchful eye of a nurse and it wouldn't do any good to stay awake worrying. Waiting up for Nicki was just plain foolishness. The young woman was eighteen years old and capable of watching out for herself. She had a key to let herself in—Deanna had made sure of that.

The house echoed with emptiness as Deanna hung her coat in the front closet. She crossed the foyer to the front door to make sure that it was locked.

As she glanced through the door's beveled glass window, her breath caught in her throat. Orangish light spilled out on the front-porch steps, revealing a man in shadows at the bottom.

A frantic voice screamed inside her head. "Go away. Leave me alone!"

Before she could move away from the door, the man came up the steps. The arc of porch light hit his face. A flood of relief overwhelmed her with such force that she was unable to get the door unlocked on the first try.

"Sorry if I startled you," Reece apologized as he stepped inside. "I couldn't sleep and was out for a walk. I saw you pull into your driveway when I was halfway down the block." His gray eyes swept her face. "I guess stopping wasn't a good idea."

"No, it's not that. I'm...I'm glad to see you." The cold had put color in his cheeks and his dark hair was in a tousled state around his face. His strong features were harmonious with his provocative, intense gaze, which had always reminded her of male models looking seductively from slick magazine ads.

"What's wrong?" he asked, touching her arm.

He was the Reece she remembered. He'd been there for her so many times that it was a natural thing for her to reach out to him for support. "It's been a hell of an evening."

"Tell me. What's going on?"

She was unable to keep her lower lip steady. "Well, for starters, it's Krissie. She had an asthma attack. I just got back from taking her to the hospital."

"Is she going to be all right?"

"She's fine, now. It's always scary when she can't get her breath." Her voice steadied a little. "I should be used to these attacks of hers, but I'm not. Anyway, I'll go get her in the morning. The doctor thought she'd have a better night's sleep if she stayed overnight. So I left her there and..." Her voice quivered and she took a deep breath. "And I was hoping Nicki would be home soon because... because..."

His gray-blue eyes held hers for a long moment. She hadn't meant to lean toward him, but she must have, for suddenly her cheek was pressed against his chest and the tears that had been gathering in her eyes spilled down her face. His strong hands splayed across her back in a gentle but firm embrace.

She closed her eyes and gave herself up to the wonderful contentment of being close to someone who had always been there for her. A moment later, they were sitting on the couch, his arm around her shoulder, and she was telling him about the hate bouquet dumped on her car.

"What's a hate bouquet?"

"Haven't you heard? Someone thought up the ghoulish idea of sending dead flowers to express malice or dislike. You know, the opposite of sending red roses as an expression of love. It's a horrible practice that seems to have caught on. But now, I'm not sure if that's what really happened. I mean, I don't know if mine was the only car covered with ugly black roses. I was too upset to do anything but get out of the parking lot as fast as I could and drive to the nearest police station." She shivered. "It was terrible having those dead flowers stuck on the wipers and windshield."

He tightened his arm around her. "What did the police do about it?"

"Nothing. The officer said it was probably college kids playing a prank. He reminded me that dead flowers were better than spray-paint graffiti." She took a deep breath and gave him a weak smile. "I really overreacted. Anyway, that's what I've been doing this evening."

REECE STUDIED her profile as she rested her head against the curve of his shoulder. Warmth swept through him as his fingers threaded the soft strands of hair. He curved his lips in a satisfied smile. For a long time, his dreams had been filled with moments like this. This is where she belonged, he thought. Always had.

"Remember the time you hurt your ankle and I had to carry you home?" he asked softly.

"And you scolded me all the way," she chided with a chuckle. "You were always giving me a bad time about something."

"And you were always hell-bent on having your own way. Dozens of times I wanted to shake some sense into you."

"Looking back, I wish you had. I'm sorry for the way I treated you before you left."

He lifted her chin with the tips of his fingers and studied her face. Telltale lines of anxiety remained around her mouth, and her blue eyes deepened darkly. He had never seen her so vulnerable. The surrendering softness of her body told him she wouldn't draw away if he kissed her. But one kiss wouldn't be enough, he knew that. Maybe it was time to—

The sound of a key in the front door decided the matter. Nicki breezed into the house, throwing her hat and jacket in one direction and her books in another. She froze when she saw him sitting on the couch with Deanna and her face registered utter surprise.

"Gee," she gasped. "I didn't mean to interrupt anything."

"You didn't," Deanna laughed, but Reece could see color sweeping up into her cheeks as she made the introductions. "This is Reece Ryndell, a childhood friend of mine. And this pretty girl is Nicki Kendall, my boarder and Krissie's baby-sitter."

"Nice to meet you," Reece said gallantly, silently cursing the interruption as he stood. He had seen Nicki at a distance but she was more attractive close up. Once he had been passing the house when she came out with her arm around the waist of a dark-haired fellow. The two of them had climbed onto a motorcycle and roared down the street. He didn't think she was the type that Deanna would like having in her house. But maybe Deanna wasn't the same girl he remembered.

He watched her as she told Nicki about Krissie's attack. From the lift of her chin and the firmness in her voice, he knew that her moment of weakness was over. Her rigid defenses were already in place again. She was in control of her emotions.

"Bummer," Nicki said. "I wished I'd been here." She glanced at Reece and he was surprised that her eyes were openly hostile. "I knew something was up with all the lights on."

"I saw them, too," Reece responded easily. "That's why I stopped."

Nicki shrugged. Then she glanced at her watch. "Gee, I didn't know it was so late. I met someone at the library and we went out for pizza."

"Well, I'm glad you're home now," Deanna said. "Did you get your research finished?"

Nicki grimaced. "I need to do a little more reading. Will you set your alarm, Dee? In case I sleep through mine?" At Deanna's nod, she said, "'Night, folks."

"Nice to meet you, Nicki," Reece offered with a smile.

She gave him a curt nod, and taking two steps at a time, she bounded up the steps.

Deanna turned to him as if she was aware of Nicki's conspicuous hostility. "I'm glad you dropped by, Reece."

"I'm glad, too." His smile broadened. "Maybe we ought to make a date to renew old times?"

He was disappointed. She refused to meet his eyes or respond to the invitation.

"I think I'd better call it a day," she said.

A surge of impatience made him swear silently as she led the way to the front door. She was as fiercely independent as she had always been.

In the foyer, he paused beside the polished black walnut newel post and glanced up the stairs at the grandfather clock sitting at an angle on the landing. "I'm glad the house is pretty much the way it always was. I always loved that clock. I remember your father winding it."

Her eyes grew misty. "It was Dad's pride and joy. He made it, you know, from a kit. Took him nearly a year to finish it."

"Did it stop working when he died, like the old song says?"

"No, something broke in it a couple of years back. I'd like to get it fixed as soon as I can afford to."

He touched her shoulder. "I'm glad you came back. This is where you belong."

Her lower lip quivered and he restrained the urge to reach for her again. "I...I wouldn't want to raise my daughter anywhere else."

How tempting it was to swing her up into his arms and carry her upstairs. *Easy does it. Tonight's a good beginning. Don't push it.*

"I'm only three blocks away," he said aloud. "Call me if you need company. Any time, day or night. Promise?"

She smiled at him. "Thanks, Reece. I promise. You're a good friend, but I need to handle things on my own."

"We'll see," he said in a prophetic tone as he went out the door.

FATIGUE ASSAULTED every inch of Deanna's body as she prepared for bed. She felt as if she'd been put through one of those old-fashioned wringers, and yet a tense wide-awake energy wouldn't let her relax.

Restlessly, she wandered around her bedroom, putting away things and getting out clothes for the next day. She was worried by the intimacy that had flared between her and Reece. For a few unguarded moments, she had reached out to him and allowed her emotions free rein. If Nicki hadn't come home, there was no telling what would have happened. The memory of his arms wrapped around her brought a warm flush to her face. He had offered a supportive strength that she desperately needed. And something more.

A dangerous awakening of sensuous feelings for him, feelings that she had thought long dead, had assaulted her. Her disastrous marriage had taught her not to trust her emotions, but a quiver of desire had raced through her as he held her. Even though he wasn't the same Reece who had been the object of her girlish adoration, he could still make her heartbeat quicken when he smiled at her with those caressing gray-blue eyes.

She set the alarm, and sat on the edge of the bed. The house was too quiet. Nicki had settled in for the night and no sounds came from Krissie's room. Restlessly, Deanna went into her daughter's room. Everything had been left in a mess in their frantic rush to the hospital. Deanna made the bed and gathered the bedtime books. She was about to put them back on the shelf when she stopped short.

The new teddy bear she had thrust into Krissie's arms just before the child had gone to sleep was not on the bed. Where was it? They had not taken it to the hospital. She'd had her hands full with Krissie and her beddie-bye blanket.

Deanna stood in the middle of the floor and let her eyes rove around the room. Then a jolt like a snap of electricity went through her.

Krissie's teddy bear was sitting primly in the rocking chair by the window—exactly the way Deanna used to place her own Winnie the Pooh bear, so long ago.

Chapter Five

Skin prickled on the back of Deanna's neck as she stared at the beady eyes of the stuffed animal looking at her from the rocking chair. For a bizarre moment, the past swept back, and the black-and-white toy changed into a golden-brown bear. Winnie the Pooh. She saw herself picking up the stuffed animal and hugging it to her chest.

But the room had been different then. The curtains, the rug and the placement of the furniture had been changed when she grew to womanhood. Since her return, when it was decided that Krissie would have Deanna's old room, the only changes she had made were shifting the bed to another wall, and placing Krissie's toys in a chest across the room. There'd never been a teddy bear of Krissie's sitting in the old rocking chair.

Deanna's mouth went dry. Had she put the teddy bear there out of habit and not remembered? All her attention had been on Krissie. In the crisis, she'd made sure that Krissie's beloved baby blanket had gone to the hospital with her, but everything else had been left behind. Try as she might, Deanna couldn't recall moving the stuffed toy. She was almost certain that the teddy bear had been left on the rumpled bed. But it couldn't have gotten from the bed to the rocking chair—*unless someone had been in the room while she was gone.*

Deanna returned to her room and sat down on the edge of the bed again. She pressed her fingers against her temples. A cold chill went up her back as she huddled there. Her thoughts whirled. The back door had been unlocked. Someone could have come in, gone upstairs and moved the teddy bear.

What nonsense! A quiver of hysterical laughter caught in her throat. Who would take the risk of being caught as a burglar just to move a toy from the bed to a chair? There had to be a sensible explanation. She had to quit putting everything in a sinister light.

If she hadn't set the teddy bear in the chair, who had? She thought for a moment. Maybe Nicki? Of course, that was it, she reasoned, feeling foolish over her paranoia. Nicki must have come into Krissie's room while she and Reece were still downstairs. Undoubtedly Nicki had started to straighten up, given up and gone off to bed.

Deanna brushed a hand across her forehead and found it beaded with perspiration. I've got to get hold of myself, she thought as she climbed into bed.

It was absurd to feel that some unnamed menace was surrounding her. She lay with the blankets pulled up to her chin and shivered from a chill that was bone-deep.

Her emotions had been on a roller coaster. Worry and anxiety had taken their toll, and she was guilty of overreacting to everything that had happened. She was certain now that the police officer was right, the bouquet of withered roses had been a sick joke. Her car had been picked at random and her reaction to the dead flowers had been way out of proportion. She hated acting like a neurotic who saw dark threats in every corner.

Even as she tried to relax, her wary nerves tightened as her ears picked up night sounds. Was that the rasp of a branch brushing against the outside brick wall? Old boards in the attic were shifting—or were those the sounds of muffled footsteps overhead? Even the wind whining at the windowpanes seemed ominous. She lay there stiff and waiting. The minutes ticked past and sleep wouldn't come.

Okay, so you're uptight, she lectured herself. No need to behave like a gothic heroine. And you're much too old to believe in the boogeyman. The mental scolding seemed to help. She turned over in the wide bed and willed herself to think of something pleasant.

Reece. Almost instantly, the remembered warmth of his arms dissipated some of the chill in the lonely bed. She remembered the caressing strokes of his hand upon her hair and the way his eyes had touched her face with that mesmerizing gaze of his. How natural it had seemed to have him in the house again.

"I'm glad the house is pretty much the way it always was," he had said. The memory of Reece looking up the stairs and commenting on the grandfather clock rose to the front of her mind. He had asked her if the clock had stopped working when her father died.

She stiffened.

The clock was set at such an angle on the landing that its face couldn't be seen from the bottom of the stairs. And yet he had known that it wasn't running. If he could see neither the silent pendulum nor the still hands on the clock, how did he know it was broken? She searched for a logical explanation. Of course, the chimes. She relaxed. Don't be a ninny. He must have missed the clock bonging the hour.

Or he had been in the house earlier.

The unbidden suspicion lurched to her mind with the scratch of a sharp nettle. Why would she think such a thing? Reece had no reason to snoop in the house when she was gone. He'd never be guilty of such duplicity. *Would he?*

She tried to suppress the suspicion, but her natural acumen wouldn't let the matter rest. What if Reece *had* been in the house earlier? And what if he *had* been in Krissie's room? He could have moved the bear from the bed to the rocking chair. The neighborhood kids had had the run of the house when she was growing up, and he would have known that she always set Pooh in the rocker.

Her mouth was suddenly dry. Maybe Reece hadn't just arrived at the house at all when she saw him on the front steps. Maybe he'd already been inside the house and had seen the lights of her car when she arrived home.

She closed her eyes tightly. Why would she even consider such an absurdity? *Because he may not be the person you remember.*

She shoved the idea away with a vicious mental thrust. She would have known if there had been a basic change in his personality. No matter what had happened to him overseas, she refused to believe that he was suffering from a sickness that went beyond the physical. She wouldn't have reacted to his touch and the softness of his voice if he hadn't been the same old Reece. He'd always been affectionate, caring and supportive, just the way he'd been with her tonight. Sure, she'd felt something stronger radiating between them, a sexual tension that hadn't been there before, but both of them had kept it under control.

Don't be an idiot, she told herself as she flounced over and beat her pillow with exasperated thumps. Now of all times when she desperately needed a strong and true friend, she'd be stupid to let her imagination put a barrier between them.

WHEN THE ALARM went off, she was positive that it couldn't be morning already. It seemed to her that she had just closed her eyes minutes before. She quickly dressed and woke up a grumpy Nicki. Nicki was definitely *not* a morning person and seldom exchanged more than a couple of words with Deanna as they passed in the hall and in the kitchen. The morning rush left little time for either of them to think about anything but the day ahead.

Nicki went out the door with a piece of toast in her mouth. Every morning she was in a frenzy, rushing to catch a ride with one of her friends to the campus. In the mayhem, Deanna completely forgot to mention the teddy bear.

She called the hospital and was assured that Krissie was ready to leave. Deanna was happy to see that her daughter was bouncing all over the hospital room when she arrived.

"She's as good as new," the doctor assured Deanna. "Don't make an invalid out of her. Let her do as much as she wants to."

Someone had given Krissie a new doll and she insisted on taking it to the day-care center with her. By the time Deanna had made the trek to the hospital, dropped off Krissie with hugs and kisses and unlocked the store, she felt as if the day should be half-over. She was still trying to get things in order for the day's business when the delivery man arrived with another shipment of pottery.

"You have to be kidding," she gasped.

"'Fraid not. Sign here, please." He stuck a clipboard into her hands.

How am I going to pay for all of this?

"Have a good day," he said as he turned on his heels and left her staring at a huge carton marked "Fragile."

When she looked at the invoice inside the box, she nearly fainted.

When Nellie came in, Deanna asked her about it.

"They never said anything to me." She shrugged her plump shoulders. "I never had much to do with anything but waiting on customers. It's awfully pretty stuff," she said, peering into the boxes. "What are you going to do with it?"

"Sell it, of course," Deanna answered rather sharply, admitting to herself that she had no idea how to market such specialized merchandise.

She went to the telephone. There was one person who might be able to help. Darrel Evans. Since he'd worked for her parents for so many years, he might know exactly why they had decided to stock up on southwest pottery.

He sounded hassled when she got him on the phone. She could picture him bouncing around, trying to do two more things while he talked to her.

"I know you're busy," she apologized, "but I'd like to set up a time to talk with you about any plans my folks had for the store."

"Sure, sure, Deanna. My pleasure. Love to help you any way I can. Unfortunately, you've caught me on a busy day. I've got to go into Denver. Let's see, tomorrow isn't good. And I'm really snowed the rest of the week.''

"It's very important," she insisted.

"Yes, yes. Well, how about . . . how about I drop by your house tonight? Say, seven o'clock?"

"That would be fine. Thanks a lot."

She had barely hung up when the telephone rang and she answered, "Dee's Candy and Gifts."

"Hi, honey. How you doing?"

Brad. The sound of his voice was a cue for a whirlwind of emotions. For a moment she couldn't think. Her hand instinctively tightened on the receiver.

"Honey, I just wanted you to know that I've got a job all lined up. Coming back to Colorado was a great idea. I guess you know I dropped by the house yesterday."

Deanna moistened her lips. "Yes, I wanted to talk to you about that. Nicki said—"

"Great little gal, Nicki," he cut in. "And is she ever crazy about you and Krissie. That's all she could talk about last night."

"What? You were with Nicki last night?" His cultivating a friendship with Nicki was the last thing she had expected—or wanted.

"Sure thing. Picked her up at the library. We went to the Sink for something to eat. Remember that place? It hasn't changed a bit since we sat in that back booth and sneaked kisses when nobody was looking."

The intimacy in his tone made her sick to her stomach. She had thought that Brad and his egotistical charm were out of her life forever. Just the sound of his voice triggered the release of remembered pain, remembered anguish and disappointment. Why couldn't he have given her more time to adjust to the challenges facing her? If he wanted to live in Boulder, that was his right and there wasn't anything she could do about it. But she wasn't going to be pulled into old patterns.

"I want to talk to you about Krissie. We have to come to some agreement about visitation," she said firmly.

"That little girl of ours is something else, isn't she? Going to turn into a little beauty," he said in a proud parental tone that Deanna had never heard before. He'd never considered fatherhood an asset in his high-profile debonair social life and had always kept himself at a distance from Krissie's daily nurturing. Now he was talking about his daughter as if she was the beginning and end of his whole life.

"You were granted weekend visitation rights twice a month," she said crisply. "Until now, you've never shown one ounce of interest in seeing Krissie. You were happy to drop out of her life and mine. I don't know what you told her, but it upset her enough that she had another asthma attack and she spent the night in the hospital."

"I just told her that Mommy and Daddy and their little girl should all be living in that house together."

"Forget it, Brad. Go home to little Miss Cheerleader."

"You've got everything wrong, Dee Dee. She was nothing to me."

"So she dumped you already? Why am I not surprised? I guess a coach without a job might have a little trouble keeping up the macho profile."

"Honest, honey, I never meant to hurt you. I can't believe you can just close me out of your life. We had five good years. A piece of paper doesn't change anything."

Deanna's temper flared. "Our marriage is over, Brad. Kaput. You're not going to wander in and out of my life whenever you feel like it. When you want to see Krissie, you make arrangements with me first. Got it? And as for Nicki, I'll fill her head so full of the truth, she'll avoid you like a case of boils." Deanna slammed down the receiver.

She was trembling. Hot, angry tears were ready to stream down her face. She turned and fled into the small bathroom at the back of the store, embarrassed that Nellie might have heard her outburst.

Splashing cold water on her face, she felt the tight knot in her stomach ease slightly. By the time she had patted her face dry and had straightened her shoulders, she could meet her reflection in the mirror with a steady eye.

All right, so you have to deal with Brad's presence for a while. She jutted her chin at the ashen face in the mirror. He can't wear you down unless you let him. She ran a comb through her hair with vigorous strokes. She'd never go back to him. Never!

When she returned to the small office, she was startled to see Reece leaning against the door frame, waiting for her.

Her emotions went into a different kind of whirl. Joyful but guarded. She wasn't sure how to react to him. Last night's suspicions lingered.

He studied her with a measured slowness that brought a flush to her cheeks. "What's going on?"

"Not much," she lied. Last night, she had been too open with him. She wasn't about to reveal the emotional garbage her ex-husband had dumped on her.

"You never were much of a liar," he said, straightening.

She gave a self-mocking laugh. He knew her too well—but did she know him? She wanted to confront him with her suspicion that he had known the clock wasn't working because he'd already made a tour of the house. She wanted to ask him if he had moved the teddy bear. But she couldn't.

A deep blue flannel shirt, matching denim jacket and slacks gave his lean body the graceful lines that she remembered so well. Waves of dark hair softened the contours of his face. Even imagining that he was capable of such deceit now seemed the height of absurdity.

"I was wondering if you'd like to come to a signing party we're having at the Dark Corner." He gave her that slow, engaging smile of his. "The guy who wrote that best seller, *Lovely, but Dead,* is going to be there tonight. I think you might enjoy it. We could go somewhere afterward and talk."

"What time?"

"Starts at seven."

For a moment, she debated calling Darrel back and canceling the meeting she had set up with him, but her conscience wouldn't let her. She had to put the store ahead of her own personal pleasures, at least until it was running smoothly.

She shook her head regretfully. "I'm sorry, I can't...tonight." She emphasized "tonight" in a way that she hoped might encourage him to ask her another time.

He opened his mouth to say something and then closed it. The black feathering in his eyes deepened, and she was sure that he was fighting back explosive anger.

"I really would like to but—"

He cut her off with a slice of his hand. "You don't have to explain. I'd forgotten how I had to get in line to spend time with the ever-popular Dee Dee. I guess things haven't changed all that much after all. Remember how you used to hurry home from an after-school date to get ready for the lucky guy who was going to take you to the movies?''

"You exaggerate," she chided.

"Do I?" he asked without a smile. "When you were in high school, there was scarcely a night that I could catch you home."

She looked at him in surprise. "I didn't know you even noticed. I mean, I didn't know you considered me anything but a neighborhood kid who was always pestering you about something."

"I admit that when you were about fifteen, you stuck to me like a cocklebur." His expression softened. "I couldn't go anywhere without you tagging after me."

"You must have known I had a terrible crush on you."

"Yes, I knew." His smile faded. "And then you grew up and fell in love with someone else." Suddenly, he was standing so close to her, she could feel his breath on her face and smell the scent of his after-shave lotion. "Why did you shut me out of your life, Dee Dee?"

As her heartbeat quickened from his nearness, it seemed impossible that she had blindly turned away from him when she met Brad. "Things just happened," she answered lamely. "All of a sudden there was this handsome football hero igniting strange and wonderful feelings that I mistook for undying love. I guess I was ready for a fairy-tale romance."

"And now?"

If he took her in his arms, she wouldn't have the will to resist him. She moved around the desk so that it was between them. "Now, I have to get my life in order."

"I see. And that doesn't include me?"

"Of course it does. Please, Reece. Give me some time."

His handsome features hardened. "The last time I gave you time to get your head on straight, you went off and got married. I'm not as patient as I was then." With that warning, he turned on his heel and left the store.

Chapter Six

Business was brisk all afternoon. Thank heavens, thought Deanna, glancing at the calendar. February the third. Only eleven days left to get rid of all the valentine stock. The ad she'd put in the *Boulder Daily Camera* seemed to be paying for itself. Nellie was ready to get off her aching feet when closing time came.

Deanna hurried home, anxious to know how Krissie had weathered the day. She silently groaned when, about a block from the house, she ran into Mrs. Caruthers, who was walking home from the supermarket. There wasn't any way for Deanna to avoid slowing her steps or offering to take one of the grocery sacks.

"Why, thank you, dear." The plump little woman gave Deanna her biggest smile.

"How are you, Mrs. Caruthers?"

"What a nice surprise. I wrote to Ellen the other day and told her you were back in Boulder. It seems like yesterday that the two of you were playing house under my kitchen table." She gave a merry laugh as she padded along beside Deanna, shifting the bulk of her weight from side to side as she walked. "What a pair you were."

Mrs. Caruthers went on to chat merrily about her daughter's marriage and move to Nebraska. Deanna made the appropriate response to the woman's chatter about her two wonderful grandsons.

"And Ellen is such a good mother," Mrs. Caruthers bragged. "Keeps a spotless house. And her little boys have such nice manners," she added in a wistful tone, probably remembering her own two little hooligans. Her eldest son, Richard, had always been beating up on his fat little brother, Benny.

Deanna remembered that Mrs. Caruthers had been an indifferent housekeeper, and a weak disciplinarian who had never had much control over Ellen or her two brothers. Mr. Caruthers spent most of his time working at his small gas station and from the woman's patter, Deanna learned that he still did.

"It's just me and Henry left. The boys moved out." She sighed. "They used to drive me crazy with all their fussing and fighting, but now I sure miss them. And Ellen and her little ones live so far away, too." Her round face brightened. "But you know how it is now that you have a little girl of your own."

Deanna nodded.

"I was asking Reece about you," she said with a fond smile. "Sometimes he stops for a chat when he's out jogging. Remember how all you kids used to have parties in our basement? I have some old photos that I bet you'd like to see. Lots of them of you and Reece. I'll bring them around sometime."

Deanna couldn't think of a polite way to tell the woman that she wasn't up to any "The Way We Were" reminiscences. Looking at old photos of happier times wasn't the way to deal with the present situation. And thinking about Reece brought forth emotions she wasn't ready to face. Things were never the same and she knew that people weren't, either. It would be easy to lean on somebody like Reece who had always been there for her, but she had to develop her own strengths.

"It's too bad what happened to Reece," Mrs. Caruthers commented as if reading Deanna's thoughts. "He's just a shadow of himself, isn't he?"

Deanna nodded. "I didn't recognize him."

"Don't know why perfectly sane people want to leave the good old U.S.A. and go traipsing off to some foreign country. They all come back changed—and not for the good, either."

Deanna left Mrs. Caruthers and her groceries at the woman's house a block away from her own, and quickened her steps the rest of the way home. She was relieved to find Krissie her usual self, bouncing around the house, leaving a trail of toys from room to room. Nicki assured Deanna that there had been no sign of any breathing problems.

"That medicine makes her hyperactive. I'm worn-out just running around after her," Nicki said with a laugh, ruffling the little girl's hair.

Deanna pulled Krissie onto her lap and nuzzled her neck while the child giggled. After several minutes, Deanna lifted the little girl off her lap.

"Take your dollies back upstairs, Krissie. Put them beddie-bye."

As soon as Krissie was out of sight, Deanna turned to Nicki. "Maybe you're worn-out because of your late night out with Brad."

"You know?"

"He called me today." Deanna's eyes flashed. "Why didn't you tell me?"

"I was going to but—but," Nicki stammered. "Gee, when I got home, that Reece was here and I didn't have a chance. And my mind was on other things this morning. Anyway, I was going to tell you tonight," she added belligerently.

"Nicki, why on earth would you go out with him?"

"Because he's a nice guy and I think it would be super if you two could get back together again. He really misses you and Krissie. That's all he talks about. Honest, Dee, I want to help if I can."

"Brad's manipulating you, using you to get to me. Our marriage is over. I have the chance now to build a life for myself and Krissie, and I'm not going to let him spoil it."

"He's not going to give up easily," Nicki warned. "I could tell that he's got his mind set."

A hard knot caught in Deanna's chest. She knew that when it came to something he wanted, Brad was as wily as the devil himself.

"Don't be mad, Dee," Nicki pleaded. "He just showed up at the library and I didn't see any harm in going for a bite to eat."

"I'm not mad." She took a deep breath and warned Nicki again that she didn't want Brad coming to the house without her permission. "Understand?"

She could tell from the way Nicki had her jaw set that the foolish girl was determined to do what she could to get Deanna to change her mind.

"I mean it, Nicki. I can't order you to stay away from Brad, but if you care anything about me and Krissie, you'll keep your distance from him."

THEY HAD JUST finished the kitchen cleanup when Darrel arrived. He blew into the living room with his usual vigor and perched on the edge of a chair as if prepared to spring to his feet at any second. His hands were a flurry of movement as he talked.

"I'm so glad you've taken over the store, Deanna. Your folks would have wanted it that way. All the years I worked for them, I heard nothing but good things about you. A perfect daughter, they always said. Of course, they were upset when your marriage failed." His bright eyes were openly curious. "I hear that your ex-hubby is back in town. Do I scent a reconciliation in the works, perhaps?''

"No."

"Oh, I'm sorry," he said as a smile creased his round face. "But then, perhaps it's for the better."

Deanna changed the subject. "I need to talk to you about the store, Darrel. Since you were with my folks for several years, I thought you might know what future plans they might have had for the business."

"I'm not sure what you mean." His broad forehead furrowed as he shifted in the chair. "Plans?"

"Did they ever talk about changing the stock in the gift section? Maybe expanding that part of the store?"

He shook his head. "I can't recall any discussions like that." His eyes were suddenly alert, like those of an animal sensing an unseen danger. "Why do you ask?"

Deanna wasn't sure how much she should tell him. After all, his store was in direct competition with hers. He might decide to restock his store to match hers. She didn't need that kind of cutthroat competition. She realized now that it hadn't been a good idea to tell him anything.

"What is it, Deanna?" His smile seemed forced. "You know I want to help you any way I can. If you have a problem—"

"No problem. I just want to follow any plans that were made for the store, and I thought you might be able to tell me what they were."

"As far as I know, your parents were happy with Dee's Candy and Gift Shop just the way it is." There was a touch of disdain in his tone. "I had some ideas that I mentioned from time to time, but they didn't want to change anything. That's why I decided to go out on my own."

Deanna nodded. "I'm sure you'll make a success of the Sweet Shoppe."

"That's it?" He looked suspicious. "That's all you wanted to ask me?"

Deanna knew then that he had expected her to pick his brain about running the store. And had the situation been different, she would have been grateful for his insights. Now, she wouldn't give him the satisfaction of knowing that she was blindly feeling her way.

"I thought . . . I thought maybe you were thinking about a merger. Or perhaps offering to let me buy you out."

She shook her head. "No, I intend to keep the store."

"It takes a lot of know-how to keep a business going. To be perfectly honest, Deanna, you don't seem the type to me." He held out his hands apologetically. "Not that you're lacking in brains. It's a matter of temperament. I just think you're ill-suited for the stresses of running a business. You have to admit that it's not easy."

"Most things in life aren't," she responded evenly.

He cleared his throat. "If we would put the two shops together, we'd have a monopoly in the mall. We could be partners."

Partners? She kept her expression bland. Partners with Darrel Evans. What a nightmare.

"I think it best that we leave things the way they are, Darrel. I have every intention of making a success of the store, just the way my parents did."

"Nothing stays the same, Deanna," he warned. He gave her a knowing smile. "You may change your mind."

"If I do, you'll be the first to know," she promised without blinking at the bald-faced lie. "Thanks for coming by, Darrel." She stood up. "I appreciate it."

"Sure, sure. Anytime. And you think about what I've said. Your parents would be pleased if I were to take over the reins of the store for you. They trusted my judgment, you know."

"Yes, I know."

She let him out the door with a sigh of relief. It had been a mistake to turn to him for help. What a waste of time. And she'd turned down an evening with Reece to boot. She glanced at her watch. Maybe it was early enough to get in on part of the book signing at the Dark Corner. Impulsively, she called the store and asked for Reece.

"Sorry, he's not here tonight," the clerk told her.

She had just hung up when Nicki came bounding down the stairs with her hat and jacket on. At the same time, a blare of a horn sounded outside. "Some of us are taking in a movie. See you later."

"Have a good time."

Nicki paused for a moment at the door. "You'll be all right, won't you?"

"Of course."

"I'm beat. I'm going to turn in early."

HE WATCHED the blond girl bound down the steps and climb into a car filled with college students. The driver made a U-turn in front of the house, and the car roared down the street and disappeared around the corner on two wheels.

She was alone with her daughter.

He was tempted to enter the house as he had done before and quietly climb the stairs to her bedroom where a muted light was shining behind a drawn drape. He had already fingered the silky under-clothes in her drawer and had raised the folds of a nightgown to his lips. Her perfume had filled his nostrils just the way it did when he stood close to her. Staring at the upstairs light, he could picture her sitting on the small stool in front of the dressing table, brushing her hair. He longed to stand behind her, thread his fingers through soft strands drifting forward around her face, and then lift her up in his arms and carry her to bed.

More than anything, he wanted to inflict the pain upon her that he had felt.

Patience, he told himself.

Valentine's Day wasn't very far away.

Chapter Seven

A thaw the next day sent the temperatures into the pleasant sixties, and Deanna felt her own spirits rise with the promise of spring. After making the daily bank deposit, she decided to stop at the bookstore to see Reece.

"You'll probably find him upstairs... far end of the building," said the college-age cashier as she let her eyes flicker over Deanna's aquamarine wool sweater, full skirt and high gray boots. "Pretty outfit."

"Thanks," Deanna said, pleased by the comment. Maybe she wasn't over the hill after all, she thought with a smile. It was nice to feel attractive once again.

Dust rose from the steps of the old stairs and mingled with the smell of musty books as she made her way to the second floor. Although a large section at the front of the store was devoted to mysteries, the majority of bookcases in the long narrow building were filled with secondhand books of every kind.

As Deanna made her way along the upper floor, she remembered the hours that she and Reece had spent looking for research material for school term papers and finding all kinds of printed treasures in the crowded racks.

They had sat Indian-style on the floor, surrounded by books and magazines, searching through the material to find what they needed. Sometimes they had read aloud to each other; other times, they'd sat quietly lost in the printed word.

When she reached Reece's hideaway in the back corner, she saw him leaning back in his chair, his feet propped up on a box and a weathered old book in his hands. She paused for a moment in the shadow of a bookcase and studied his profile. His recent illness had left a gauntness that only emphasized the strong planes in his face and his deep-set gray eyes. She was aware of his rugged independence, his determination to be what he wanted to be. As her eyes swept over the sensuous length of his body, she felt a quivering response to his maleness.

At the sound of her breathing, he slowly turned around. For a moment, his expression remained the same, pensive, studied and guarded. Then a veil lifted from his eyes and he smiled at her. "What brings you to this dusty old corner?" he asked as he stood up.

"I felt the need of...of...something to read."

"Really?"

"Yes." She knew that her eyes gave him a different answer. *I wanted to see you.*

"Well, now, we might be able to find a book or two to interest you." His voice softened as his gaze locked with hers. "Are you after something scientific or something on the lighter side?"

"I'm not sure." Her voice was suddenly husky.

With a fingertip he lifted a wisp of hair from her cheek and eased it back behind her ear. His touch lingered. "As I recall, you're something of a romantic in your tastes."

"Yes," she said softly. "I'm afraid I am."

"Nothing to be afraid of." He reached out and took her hands gently in his. "May I make a suggestion?"

She wanted to say something light and facetious but her breath had caught like a trapped butterfly in her throat. For a long moment, a wordless communication flared between them as they stood there with her hands captured in his.

Slowly he drew her to him.

She could have easily pulled away, turned her head, or done a dozen other things, but she didn't. She lifted her face to his.

His kiss was gentle at first as he pressed his mouth against hers in a cautious meeting. But as a fiery charge burst from the contact and the pressure of his kisses increased, she felt a hunger that dismayed her.

Even the layer of clothes between them could not diffuse the heat.

"Dee Dee," he murmured as he rained kisses on her cheeks, her mouth and the soft skin showing in the V of her pullover sweater.

Frightened by her own abandoned response to his kisses, she tried to pull back, but he held her firmly. From the depths of an exploding passion came a quiver of fright. She was being swept away into dangerous waters by someone who had always been her safe haven.

As if sensing her panic, he released her. For a long moment, they stood there, staring at each other, breathing heavily. Then a wry smile curved the corners of his lips. "That wasn't the suggestion I was going to make. Honest."

She searched his face. Nothing was showing but a questioning wonder. He must have been as surprised as she at the desire that had lain dormant all these years. She gave him a self-conscious grin. "And what were you going to suggest?"

"That it's time we do something besides reading."

"I think you made your point," she said wryly.

They shared a breathless laugh.

"I was going to call you this morning," he said, easing back on the corner of his desk and swinging his leg slightly.

She began to relax. His body language told her that he wasn't going to touch her again despite the charged attraction still snapping between them.

"Really? Well, I called you at the store last night," she confessed. "Things worked out so I was free earlier than I thought."

He frowned. "I wish I'd known. I decided to pass up the signing. Spent the evening asleep in front of the boob tube. I hope I haven't completely scuttled any chances of your going out with me."

Even as an inner voice told her to give herself some time to adjust to the idea of Reece as a lover instead of a platonic friend, she found herself saying, "I'd like to go out with you."

His expression eased. "Good. How about tomorrow night? There's a new place just opened up, called the Silver Spur. Terrific barbecue menu and a western band for dancing. Remember when you taught me the latest steps in the Carutherses' basement?"

Deanna laughed. "We had some good times, didn't we? I saw Mrs. Caruthers yesterday. She says she's going to bring some photos by the house. I bet they'll bring back a lot of memories." Once again, the lyrics of the song "The Way We Were" came to mind. *"Water-colored memories."* Is that what they were? Too faded to remember clearly?

"What's the matter? Suddenly you look sad. Is that the reaction you have to going dancing with me?" he chided.

"No, of course not. It's a date. *If* Krissie is feeling well and *if* I can get Nicki to baby-sit. Most Saturday nights she's busy, but I think she might agree to stay with Krissie tomorrow."

"Great. Seven o'clock, all right?"

"Fine. Now I really have to get back to the store."

"I'll walk to the front with you."

"No need," she said quickly. "I know my way."

She didn't want him to walk her out of the store. He might take her arm or press close to her as they maneuvered through the small aisles between the book racks, and she was still reeling from their encounter. She wondered if her face was as flushed as it felt. Could anyone tell that her lips were soft and warm from his passionate kisses?

"See you tomorrow night, then." He stayed seated on the corner of his desk. She felt his intense gaze upon her back as she quickly walked away.

ON SATURDAY, the sale of valentine candy and gifts kept the cash register ringing. Deanna was too busy to think much about her date with Reece. She was relieved that the busy holiday was going to bring in needed profit.

Nicki had agreed to baby-sit, but when she found out who Deanna's date was, she didn't try to hide her disappointment. Nicki wanted Deanna to be going out with Brad.

"I told you that's over!" Deanna said sharply. "I'm never going back to him."

"Well, there's something about Reece that I don't like,", she said honestly. "I don't trust guys with hooded eyes."

"They're not hooded," Deanna protested.

"Maybe not on the outside," Nicki said with a toss of her blond hair. "But you can't see what he's thinking. I don't know, I just have the feeling he's dissecting me into little pieces when he looks at me. I'd never date a guy like that."

"You'd prefer someone like Tony who leaves a valentine pinned to the door with a butcher knife?"

"Oh, he didn't do it. I asked him."

Deanna swallowed hard. "Then who did?"

She shrugged. "Beats me."

Deanna's hands tightened at her sides. "Tony must have done it. He's lying about it. I can't think of anybody else who would play such a sick joke."

"I can," Nicki said pointedly.

Deanna didn't need to ask who she had in mind, but she dismissed the inference as nonsense. The ugly incident had Tony's name written all over it.

REECE WAS LATE picking her up. Deanna wandered through the living room, nervously gathering stray toys and fluffing sofa pillows. Several times she glanced at her reflection in a gilded mirror and paused to smooth her hair and straighten the collar of her blouse. As she stilled a nervous quiver, she laughed. *What's the matter with you? You're as keyed up as a girl waiting for her first date.*

Well, in a way, this was a first date, she reasoned. Although she and Reece had done hundreds of things together, tonight was different. They were no longer just friends. The passion that had flared between them made everything different, more uncertain— and dangerous.

Forty-five minutes later, he arrived. She thought he looked like a model for a Marlboro advertisement, ruggedly handsome in western pants and a fringed tan shirt outlining his tall frame. "Sorry, I got held up at the store," he apologized.

She passed off his tardiness as unimportant and tried to give the impression that she hadn't even noticed the time. "Nicki's upstairs reading to Krissie. I was glad to have a little time to straighten up the house."

His hands lingered on her shoulders as he helped her into her winter coat. "Hmm, you smell nice," he said, close to her ear. "I'm glad you haven't changed your perfume."

The slight pressure of his fingers caused her to lean back against him, and she felt the warmth of his breath as he placed a kiss on the nape of her neck. She closed her eyes for a moment. It had been such a long time since she'd felt so utterly, wonderfully feminine.

They talked very little on the way to the Silver Spur, and once they had entered the crowded western bar, there was too much noise for casual conversation. In a way, she was glad. It was enough that they were seated close together at a small round table, exchanging amused glances as they ate and licked sauce off their fingers.

A lot of people seemed to know Reece and a pert bleached-blond waitress engaged him in flirtatious banter. He must be a regular, Deanna decided, surprised. She couldn't remember Reece ever being a guy who liked boisterous nightlife.

His dancing had improved so much that she was challenged to keep up with him as he laced her arms above their heads in fancy twists and turns. The dance floor was filled with couples doing the two-step around the room, and she was dizzy when he finally swung her into her chair at the end of a Garth Brooks tune.

"You're wonderful," she gasped. She couldn't believe this was the same long-legged fellow she'd taught to dance during neighborhood parties.

"I've been taking lessons," he said solemnly. "To get ready."

"For what?"

"For when you came home and I could take you dancing."

A flicker of uneasiness made her ask, "How did you know I'd be coming back?"

His compelling gaze locked with hers. "Let's just say I know you better than you know yourself. Come on, love." He grabbed her hand. "I want to show you what I can do with a polka."

Laughing, they bounced through a western polka and followed it with the country swing. He held her close as the tempo slowed to a ballad sung by a husky-voiced baritone lamenting the loss of his true love. Reece's hand on her back held her firmly against him. She closed her eyes and let the romantic music weave a spell around her as they moved together. He lowered his hands to her waist and guided her hips in a motion that was boldly seductive and tantalizing. When the music ended, his arms tightened around her and they stood together in the middle of the dance floor for a long moment before he stepped away and guided her back to their table.

All evening she felt strangely renewed. She laughed and talked with a spontaneity she hadn't known for years. She hadn't realized how her unhappy marriage had withered her spirit. Being with Reece made her feel as if her youth had been given back to her.

"Having a good time?" he asked as if the glow in her face wasn't answer enough.

"Wonderful! I'd forgotten how much fun dancing could be—"

"With the right person," he finished.

She smiled at him. "Yes, with the right person."

"I've always been the right person for you, Dee Dee. Didn't you know that?" He put his hand possessively over hers. "Why don't you admit that it's time we did something about it?"

Her smile wavered. She withdrew her hand. "I'm not ready to make another commitment. It's too soon. I need some time."

"How much time?"

"I don't know."

She saw the shutter that Nicki had described come down over his eyes. Was he hurt, angry—or hiding some other emotion she didn't understand?

"Will you excuse me a minute?" Weaving through the crowd, she made her way to the ladies' room. She stared at her flushed face in the mirror and chided herself for holding Reece at arm's length when every sensory bud in her body blossomed when he touched her. Why couldn't she let herself go? What stiff-necked pride kept her from admitting that he could provide a support that she desperately needed? It was stupid to keep wavering between trust and doubt. She freshened her lipstick with a firm hand. She would quit fighting the feelings he aroused in her. She was lucky to have found someone who could make her believe in love again.

By the time she returned to the table, he had finished his drink and was smiling at her as if there had never been any discord between them. "Come on, let's try a square dance."

A few minutes later when they were sitting down again, catching their breaths, the blond waitress came over to their table.

"Are you Deanna Donovan?" She held out a red envelope. "Somebody left this at the desk for you."

Deanna stared at her name printed in bold letters on the front. All warmth left her body and her hand trembled as she tore open the envelope and drew out a pretty valentine. A message was scribbled under the card's flowery verse.

Foxy, you'd better get back to your candy store. And fast.

Chapter Eight

Music, clinking glasses and laughter roared through Deanna's head like a hurricane. All thought was lost in a swell of emotion that left her trembling.

"What is it?" Reece took the valentine from her hand, read it and then swung around to the waitress. "Where'd you get this?"

The girl raised a plucked eyebrow. "I told you, someone left it at the desk. I didn't see who it was, though," she answered defensively. "I figured your date must be Deanna Donovan since you'd been calling her Dee Dee all evening. So some secret admirer left her a valentine. What's the big deal?" She shrugged her plump shoulders and strode away.

Foxy. The name whirled in her head.

"Do you know who sent it?" Reece asked.

"It must be that man...."

"What man?"

"A guy who followed me home one night. He called me Foxy." She turned to Reece. "Do you think he's done something to the store?"

"There's only one way to find out." Reece grabbed Deanna's hand and led her through the crowded bar to a pay-phone in the foyer. "We'd better alert the police. They can get to the store sooner than we can."

Fear brought hot beads of sweat to Deanna's forehead. She'd forgotten all about the man in the old blue Chevy. Could it be the same person? Or had she told someone about the incident, someone who was using the name to frighten her? But who? It must be the same man. But how could he have known where to find her unless he'd followed her to the Silver Spur?

She instinctively pressed against the wall as Reece talked to someone at the police station. There were people everywhere, coming and going, standing in groups or alone. Her frightened gaze traveled over everyone she could see. Several men met her eyes. Some looked away. And some sent her a knowing smile. They all blended together in a rise of panic. *Dear God, was he staring into her eyes at that moment?* And what had he done to the store? Was it already engulfed in flames?

"They'll check it out," Reece said, hanging up. "Probably only a sick joke."

"But who would do it?"

He shrugged. "Anyone could have left the envelope at the counter."

The way he dismissed the matter fired her suspicions. *Even you!* She'd been in the ladies' room for several minutes. He could have left the table and furtively put the envelope on the counter.

He took her arm. "We'd better do as the card says. Don't look so frightened. It'll be all right, love," he said soothingly. He slipped a protective arm around her waist, and the wonderful intimacy that had been between them all evening flared again, mocking her ridiculous suspicions.

Reece drove at the speed limit from the outskirts of Boulder to downtown. Sitting close to him, Deanna tried to remember if she'd told him about the night the old blue car had followed her home. She had a vague memory that she'd mentioned it to him.

"No, you didn't tell me," Reece said when she asked him.

"He stalked me in his car when I was coming home about midnight from the store. He called me Foxy. When I wouldn't get into the car with him, he nearly ran it up on the sidewalk as he followed me all the way home."

"And you didn't see who it was?"

"No, it was too dark and the windows were dirty." She swallowed against the tightness in her throat. "He must have followed us to the bar and left the envelope at the desk when no one was looking."

She expected to hear the sound of sirens as they approached the side street leading to the mall, but there were only the usual muffled sounds of cars and pedestrians. Reece drove down the alley behind the store, and pulled up beside a police car parked at the back door. Nothing looked out of the ordinary.

Just as Deanna and Reece got out of the car, two officers finished circling the building.

"You called in the report?" asked a gray-haired cop who introduced himself as Sergeant McDowell and his young partner as Jim Hanks.

Reece nodded. "This is Deanna Donovan, the owner. Someone left this at the Silver Spur for her." He handed the officer the valentine.

Sergeant McDowell directed his flashlight at the card and read the message. Then he gave a deep-throated snort and handed the card to his partner. "Foxy, is it?"

Deanna felt the color sweep up into her cheeks as the two officers exchanged knowing grins.

"Any idea which boyfriend might have sent it?" asked the young curly-haired officer.

Reece put a warning pressure on Deanna's arm, staying her explosive retort as he succinctly related the stalking incident. "Sounds like the same jerk," Reece said. "Intent on harassing her."

"A stalker, huh?" Both policeman had sobered. "Have you seen the same car any time since?"

"No, but I thought someone was following me the other night...when I left the hospital. But I didn't see the car and...and I'm not sure."

"Well, there's no sign of a break-in. Probably the guy's just jerking your string," offered the youthful Hanks.

"Give me your key, Mrs. Donovan. We'd better take a look inside. You wait here," McDowell ordered.

Reece kept his arm around Deanna's waist. The five-minute wait seemed like an eternity. When the young patrolman came out of the back door, she could tell from his expression that the officers had found something.

"What is it?" she croaked. Had someone else been killed in the store?

Reece must have been thinking along the same lines. "Did you find a body?"

"No, nothing like that," Hanks assured him, waving them in. He directed them to the small storeroom at the back of the store. "Just vandalism."

Deanna stood in the doorway of the storage room and stared in disbelief. Boxes had been thrown off the shelves and all the contents emptied. Jagged shards of the lovely earthenware pottery were scattered in every direction. Cardboard boxes had been trampled. Small racks had been overturned. An earthquake couldn't have wreaked any more havoc than the unseen hand that had smashed all the dinnerware, bowls and vases beyond recognition.

The vandalism was shocking enough, but in the midst of the destruction someone had placed the large teddy bear from the window display. The stuffed animal held out its arms to them.

The red ribbon Deanna had tied around its neck was still there. But its head had been chopped off.

Chapter Nine

As Deanna stared at the decapitated stuffed animal, the red ribbon gave her the impression of fresh blood. A weakness developed in her legs. She must have wavered, because Reece's arm went around her waist. "Come on. You need to sit down."

He led her across the hall to her office. She eased into a chair and put her head in her hands. Then she looked up at him with wounded eyes. "Why would anyone do something like that?"

He shook his head as he handed her a glass of water.

"I don't understand it. I don't understand it at all. How did he get in?"

"He must have had a key."

Her eyes widened.

"What is it?" he asked as he saw her expression.

She was remembering the night the valentine had been pinned to her door and Nicki's explanation about Tony taking her keys for the prank. She told

Reece about the incident. "Nicki says he swears he didn't do it but I think he's lying. I've never liked the guy and I've let Nicki know that I don't think she should be dating him."

"Maybe he's trying to get back at you for interfering in his love life."

"He could have gotten my keys at some time and made copies," she continued thoughtfully. "Do you think I ought to tell the police?"

Before Reece could answer, Sergeant McDowell came into the office with his notebook open. His first question was whether someone might have a grudge against her.

Deanna opened her mouth and then closed it. She couldn't point her finger at Tony. Nicki would never forgive her if she turned him in to the police. Besides, she had nothing but her own dislike of him on which to base her suspicions.

She shook her head and sent a warning look to Reece not to tell the officer what she had been saying about Tony. "Her ex-husband could have done it," Reece said, avoiding Deanna's eyes.

She wanted to laugh. The idea that Brad was responsible for such an act of destruction was ridiculous. That wasn't his way. Even when he was angry, he used his charm to manipulate and to control. "Brad would never go to such lengths to make me angry," she countered. "He can do that with a few words."

"Does he have a key to the store?" McDowell asked.

"No."

"You're sure? Could he have had access to one?"

She blanched. Brad had been in the house. Her parents had left a ring of spare keys hanging in the kitchen. She hadn't even checked to see if one of them belonged to the store. The officer just nodded when she told him about the extra keys.

"And your ex-husband would have known about the keys?" As she nodded, he asked for Brad's name and whether she knew where he was staying.

"No, I don't."

"Then you're not in contact with your ex-husband?"

"No more than I can help."

"But you have been in touch with him recently." At her nod, he asked, "How recently?"

"This past week. I talked to him on the phone."

"But he hasn't been to your house or had access to the extra keys?"

She bit her lower lip. "Brad was at the house... when I wasn't home. I suppose he could have lifted a key from the kitchen ring."

Deanna's conviction that Brad wasn't the guilty party began to waver.

"We will need to talk with your ex-husband, Mrs. Donovan. If you find out where he's staying, let us know." He went back over the story of the man who had stalked her. "Are you sure it wasn't someone you know?"

"I'm not sure of anything," she admitted. There was no way to prove that Tony had put the vile valentine on her door or stolen her keys.

The officer frowned. "A few months ago, your parents were shot during a robbery."

"Do you think the two incidents are related?" Reece asked.

"Not likely, but who knows? I'll see if we can put some surveillance on your house and the store for a while, Mrs. Donovan. I'll have a patrol car put both of them on its nightly route. Maybe we'll be lucky and come up with something. And you'd better have the locks changed first thing Monday morning."

The officer asked a few more questions and then told her to go home.

"I'd better clean up this mess first," she protested.

"No, don't. Leave it as it is for now. We may want to come back tomorrow to dust for fingerprints."

"It'll wait until Monday," Reece assured her as he led her away from the storeroom.

She rested her head against his shoulder for a brief moment, then took a deep breath and straightened up. By the time Reece stopped the car in front of the house, anger had replaced Deanna's bewilderment. She was fuming inside. Such wanton destruction made her itch to get her fingers around the throat of the perpetrator.

"I wish I had caught him in the act. I'd have broken the nearest pot over his head," she said as they went inside the house.

As he helped her off with her coat, Reece gave a wry laugh but there was no mirth in it. Deanna looked at him. Deep shadows across his eyes masked his thoughts. She had the weird impression that the vandalism hadn't surprised him as much as it should have. Suddenly, his manner seemed calculating and wary.

Her thoughts sped back over the evening. Reece had been late picking her up. He said he had been detained at the store.

An inner voice mocked, *Which store?*

No, she couldn't suspect him.

Why not? He could have easily left the valentine at the Silver Spur desk at some time during the evening. Maybe he knew all along what the police would find. *Stop it!* This was crazy. She put a hand to her forehead. Her thoughts blocked out his voice as she tried to subdue a growing uneasiness.

"What?" she asked when she realized he was waiting for an answer.

"I said, I think I should move in with you. Until this weirdo is caught."

She blinked. "Move in with me?"

"Don't look so horrified." He put his hands on her shoulders. "You have an extra bedroom. I'm *only* suggesting your having a man's protection while this nut is running loose." His hands slipped gently down her arms. "Although I must admit there might be some fringe benefits to the arrangement."

She stepped back. Anger glowed in her eyes like banked red coals. "Thank you for your offer but when any man moves in with me, it will be at *my* invitation."

"I didn't mean—"

"I can't handle anything more tonight, Reece," she said, cutting him off.

Maybe she was being overly sensitive about his suggestion. On the surface, it seemed a sensible precaution. She had the extra room and some of the loneliness she'd felt since her divorce would be eased. She was weary with the twenty-four-hour responsibility for the house, her daughter and her boarder. Her feelings for Reece were anything but platonic— and maybe that was the problem. A developing love affair could be destroying her good judgment. She had to be sure of him and of herself before committing to anything as intimate as having him living with her.

REECE GRIPPED the steering wheel with white-knuckled hands as he drove away, furious with himself. He'd had such great plans for the whole evening and he'd blown it. He could still see the shock in her eyes when he had suggested that he move in with her.

Damn it, he swore. She should have been ready to reach out to him. Instead, she was reeling from the shock of the vandalism.

The evening had gone wonderfully while they were eating and dancing at the Silver Spur. She'd been surprised at his new man-about-town image. He could tell she was looking at him with new eyes. Maybe if he'd learned how to have a good time when she had been ready to fall in love, he wouldn't have lost her to that bastard, Donovan.

He took a deep breath and tried to relax. All of that was in the past, he told himself. It was the present that he had to deal with. His darling Dee Dee wasn't going to get away from him again. When he had held her, seductively swaying to the music and fitting the sweet length of her body against his, he had wanted her as he had never wanted a woman. All the tender feelings he had been holding back had surfaced, demanding release—soon.

His thoughts spun ahead to Valentine's Day.

DEANNA CONCENTRATED her energies the next day on managing Krissie and taking care of household chores like shopping and cleaning. She was glad that she had something to keep her busy since activity kept worrisome thoughts at the back of her mind. She was almost able to ignore those that crept forward demanding attention. Thoughts about Reece were the hardest to control. She wanted to think about him, to remember the wonderful moments in his arms. He could have been with her this very moment, she tortured herself as she loaded the washing machine.

On one level, she wanted to give in to the temptation to open up her life to him. Last night had been wonderful. Dancing. Laughing together. Feeling that breathless sensation when they looked at each other. How easily they were able to build on a deep affection that had always been there. *Then why the hesitation?* Her apprehension was foolish. Irrational. But it was a warning lurking in some deep crevice of her mind.

At breakfast, she told Nicki that someone had broken into the store. The girl's pretty blue eyes widened. "Did they cart off all the candy?"

Deanna repressed a smile, certain that Nicki's sweet tooth had prompted the question.

"Nothing was taken. And no damage was done to the front of the store, thank heavens. Only boxes in the storeroom were broken open and their contents smashed to bits. And...and..." Her voice faltered. "And he cut off the head of the big teddy bear from the window display."

Nicki grimaced. "Gross! Somebody must have been on a bad trip. I wonder why he picked your store."

Deanna didn't answer.

"Do the police have any ideas?"

"No." Deanna was tempted to confess that Tony was at the top of her list. But what good would that do? She'd already been pretty vocal about her dislike of Nicki's volatile boyfriend. She didn't want to alienate the girl, but she needed some answers.

"Have you seen Tony lately?" she asked a little while later, as casually as she could.

Fortunately, Nicki didn't seem to connect this train of thought with Deanna's earlier suspicions. "No. We had a bummer of a fight. I told him I didn't want to see him again."

"Did you mention my name? I mean, you didn't tell him that I had been trying to get you to break up with him, did you?"

Nicki shrugged. "I might have. We went at it fast and furious for a while. What a swelled head. He couldn't believe that I'd dump him. Anyway, it's all over." She gave Deanna her sweet smile. "I knew you'd be happy."

A weight settled on Deanna's shoulders. She hadn't liked Tony but she had no right to run Nicki's life to please herself. Maybe she should have kept her mouth shut and not tried to influence Nicki against him. Well, it was too late for regrets. If Tony was trying to get even, he'd chosen an especially nasty way to do it.

"You are glad, aren't you?" Nicki asked, obviously puzzled by Deanna's expression.

"Yes, of course," she answered quickly. "I think you can do better."

Nicki tossed her blond head. "And I think you can do better than that Reece fellow. Are you gone on him?"

"No, of course not," Deanna answered defensively. "He's just an old friend. We had a good time last night until ... until I got that horrid valentine. I checked the key ring in the kitchen, but I don't have any idea how many keys my parents left there. Someone could have taken a key to get into the store, and I wouldn't know it."

Nicki raised her eyebrow. "Who would swipe a key?"

"Maybe Brad. Was he in the kitchen the other day when he stopped by?"

"Sure. He said he'd always loved the place. He talked about the good times you used to have when you were dating. He wandered all over with a sad look on his face. You're not thinking he had anything to do with vandalizing the store, are you?" she asked, frowning.

"No, of course not. It was just that Reece—" she broke off.

"Oh, sure, he'd love to point the finger at Brad," she scoffed. "Anything to keep you two apart."

Deanna disliked the direction the conversation was going, so she asked, "What are you going to do today?"

Sunday was the only day in which Nicki was completely free of her baby-sitting duties.

"Some of us are going up to Boulder Canyon and do a little rock climbing." A honking horn followed her words. "Got to go!" She scrambled to collect her things and then barreled out the front door.

"Be careful," Deanna called after her and then chided herself for being such a mother hen.

KRISSIE TOOK a nap right after lunch. Deanna was sitting in the living room when the doorbell rang. *Reece.* Her heartbeat quickened. She was ashamed of her abruptness last night and he'd been at the edge of her thoughts all day. In the light of day, her paranoia was almost laughable. She gave her hair a smoothing swipe and hurried to the front door. The smile on her lips faded.

Tony DeVargas stood there.

"Nicki isn't here." Deanna stepped back, ready to close the door, but he was inside before she could move.

"I came to see *you.*"

A white-toothed smile shone in his olive-tan face. As he looked at her, his leer stripped away her cotton shirt and shorts, and gave her the horrid sensation that she was standing naked before him. This wasn't the first time he'd made her uncomfortable, but today the determined glint in his eyes frightened her. "Please leave," she said in a firm voice.

His laugh was mocking. "I think it's time we got better acquainted—now that you've broken up Nicki and me."

"I had nothing to do with that."

He just smiled as if to say that they both knew it for a lie. "It's time for you to pay up."

Don't let him see your fear. She remembered that admonition from a lecture on self-defense. Good advice, but how could she hide her fright when he could draw a knife or a gun on her at any second?

"Get out of my house—*now,*" she managed to say. "If you don't, Tony, I'll call the police."

Her mind raced. Could she outrun him if she shoved him aside and darted up the stairs? Could she reach a telephone? Find a weapon?

"And what will you tell the cops? That I came to collect my girl and you went all hysterical on me?"

"I'll tell them you threatened me."

"But I haven't, have I?" he asked in a reasonable tone that was at odds with his thick hands that were suddenly on her waist. "We've never had a chance to really talk."

"Take your hands off me."

He brought his face close to hers.

She jerked her head to one side. "Don't make a fool of yourself, Tony."

He gave a husky laugh. "Now why don't you and I just take a walk upstairs and—"

The doorbell cut off his next word.

Tony swore. Then he seemed to get control of himself. As he dropped his hands, Deanna's body went slack with relief.

"Yoo-hoo," Mrs. Caruthers called through the half-opened door. "Yoo-hoo, Deanna. It's me. I brought the photos for you to look at."

Chapter Ten

Deanna called loudly, "Come in, Mrs. Caruthers. Come in."

The front door opened all the way. "Oh, you have company. I'll come back—"

"No. It's all right," Deanna said, moving quickly and taking the woman's arm. "I'm glad you came by."

You don't know how glad.

Tony brushed by the two women and slammed the front door behind him as he left.

"Oh, my," Mrs. Caruthers said with a nervous titter, "I'm afraid I've come at a bad time."

"Not at all," Deanna assured her. "You couldn't have timed your visit better."

"Who is that young man? I've seen him in the neighborhood quite a lot."

"I have a college student living with me. And he's her boyfriend. I mean, he was. They've broken up."

"Oh, that's why he reminded me of a tomcat with his tail caught in the door." Mrs. Caruthers looked relieved. "I was afraid I'd interrupted something between the two of you." She eyed Deanna. "You both looked rather...intense."

"He was making himself obnoxious," Deanna admitted. "I think he blames me for the breakup."

"Well, well. Young love never did run smooth," she quoted with a broad smile. "I used to tell Ellen that the right man would come along. And when Homer came calling, I knew he was the one. You've never met him, have you? He's the—"

"Come on into the living room." Deanna was determined not to show how shaken she was. "We can sit down and you can tell me more about Ellen and her family."

Her heartbeat was still racing and her knees weak. As they sat on the sofa, she was glad that there was no need for her to make conversation. Mrs. Caruthers launched into a tale about Ellen's courtship and marriage, painting her son-in-law as a modern knight who had swept her darling daughter off her feet. Deanna listened and hoped that Ellen was as happily married as her mother declared. Knowing Ellen as she did, Deanna suspected that she might have married just to get away.

"With so many marriages ending in divorce," Mrs. Caruthers said pointedly, "I feel very lucky that *my* daughter is one of the happy ones."

Deanna smiled inwardly. Ellen had missed out on a lot of dates while Deanna had enjoyed teenage popularity. Apparently Mrs. Caruthers thought it was time to even the score.

"I'm glad Ellen's happy," Deanna said honestly. "She deserves the best."

"Neither of my boys have married," Mrs. Caruthers said regretfully. "But Ellen has made me a happy grandmother." She fished in a large, worn purse and brought out an envelope of photos. The first half-dozen were of Ellen and a bashful beanpole husband on their wedding day. In a family picture, Mr. Caruthers looked the same as Deanna remembered, disorientated, as if the glowing bride and his two scowling overweight sons, Richard and Benny, belonged to somebody else.

Then Mrs. Caruthers began handing Deanna pictures taken over several years at various neighborhood gatherings. They spanned the years from grade school to the year Deanna had met Brad and put the neighborhood and everyone in it out of her life.

In almost every photo, Deanna was standing next to Reece. She'd forgotten how tall and good-looking he had been. She could remember how she'd always played up to him, trying to monopolize his attention even though she was just a kid, four years his junior. Old feelings rushed back as she looked at the photos.

"Here's one taken at a Halloween party," Mrs. Caruthers said. "You and Ellen must have been about fourteen in that picture. Dressed like a southern belle, you were. Don't you remember? Reece went to some store in Denver and rented the costume for you.''

Deanna stared at the picture of herself, looking saucily at the camera and holding a lacy parasol over her shoulder. She'd forgotten all about the lovely lavender dress with its hoopskirt. Reece had brought the umbrella and dress to the house the day before Halloween. ''You always said you wanted to be Scarlett O'Hara,'' he had told her.

Her eyes grew misty, remembering.

''You didn't need an older brother with Reece around,'' Mrs. Caruthers said. ''He sure looked after you.''

''Yes, he did,'' she agreed softly. *And he still wants to look after me.* She gave Mrs. Caruthers a grateful smile. ''Thanks for letting me see the pictures. I think they've helped me straighten out some things in my own mind.''

''You just keep them. Maybe you want to put them in an album or something. I always meant to.'' She sighed. ''But I never will. And neither will Ellen. She's too busy with her family. And the boys don't care about them.'' She sighed again. ''Sometimes I wish the house was filled with all the daily confusion again. Life gets pretty lonesome with all the kids gone.''

Deanna was about to respond just as she heard pattering footsteps on the stairs. Krissie peeked through the banister into the living room. Her daughter was up from her nap.

"Come on down, darling," Deanna urged with a smile. "There's a nice lady here to see you."

Krissie's hair was tumbled around her face in moist brown curls, and her deep blue eyes were still a little heavy from her nap as she came into the room. She clutched the white teddy bear as Deanna swept the child into her arms. It was her turn to show off her pride and joy.

"This is Krissie, my three-year-old."

"My, my, she's a beautiful little angel," Mrs. Caruthers cooed. She dived into her bottomless purse and brought out a roll of candy. "I always keep them for the little ones," she said with a self-conscious smile.

Impulsively, Deanna invited Mrs. Caruthers to the kitchen to share the afternoon snack of cookies and milk that Krissie always had after her nap.

The older woman beamed and readily accepted. Deanna was grateful for her company. The next hour passed quickly as Mrs. Caruthers reminisced about many of the things that Deanna had forgotten.

"Well, I guess I'd best be going."

"I'm glad you came. Please drop by again." The visit had allowed Deanna to put Tony's frightening advances at the back of her mind.

"I enjoyed it, dear. Took me back, it did." Mrs. Caruthers's shoulders slumped and her footsteps slowed as she walked to the front door. "I'll be sure and tell Ellen that I saw you."

Deanna touched the older woman's arm. "I wonder if you might baby-sit Krissie for me sometime, Mrs. Caruthers?"

Her round face brightened. "Why, of course, I would," she said in a rush, giving Deanna a hug. "Anytime. Anytime, at all."

After her neighbor had gone, the ugliness of Tony's visit came back. What would have happened if Mrs. Caruthers hadn't arrived, Deanna wondered. Should she report the incident to the police? Tony would never admit that he'd made a pass at her, and her accusations might make her look like some neurotic female. On the other hand— Krissie tugged at her sleeve. "Park, Mommy. Teddy wants to swing."

Deanna had been taking Krissie to a neighborhood park every Sunday afternoon that the weather would allow. This had been their private time together and Deanna had been careful not to let anything interfere with it.

"All right, honey. Let Mommy change clothes first."

They walked the three blocks to the park and joined a number of parents and children enjoying the playground on this springlike day. Skipping beside Deanna, Krissie chattered in her fractured sentence structure about everything that caught her interest.

Deanna laughed and tried to answer all her questions.

Breathing in brisk fresh air under a Colorado blue sky, she felt her frayed nerves begin to knit. She'd always possessed a natural resilience that had allowed her to bounce back after any defeat. Her parents had called this trait a willful stubbornness. Now, Deanna was grateful for it.

She didn't see anyone that she knew at the park, nor on the way home—until she turned the corner of her block.

"Hey, wait up!" Reece jogged toward them from across the street. His face was flushed and the band that held his dark hair back from his forehead was moist with sweat. For a moment, she was swept into one of the photos that had shown Reece holding up a ribbon he'd won at a high-school track meet. Running was the only thing Reece had ever been competitive about.

"I stopped by to see you but nobody was home."

"We went to the park."

"I thought so. That's where I was headed."

Reece matched his steps to Deanna's as they continued along the sidewalk. Krissie went skipping ahead, playing some kind of game of jump-over-the-cracks.

"How are you?" he asked.

She avoided looking directly at him. "Fine."

"Fine?" He gave her one of his persuasive smiles. "Then why do you have that telltale tightness at the corner of your mouth?" he asked softly.

"I don't!" she snapped and then caught herself. Why be so defensive? She didn't have to pretend the way she had with Brad. This wasn't her juvenile husband she was talking to, but an old and trusted friend. "I'm sorry," she apologized. "I didn't mean to be so sharp with you. Force of habit, I'm afraid."

"Don't apologize. I know you're under a lot of pressure. I wish you'd let me help."

"What can you do? It's all so bizarre."

"I could be there for you." He took her hand and held it warmly in his. "Did you think over my offer to be a live-in bodyguard?"

Relieved to be sharing the ugly incident with someone, she told him about Tony. "I could have used one earlier this afternoon," she admitted. "I've always felt uncomfortable around Nicki's boyfriend, but I never expected him to come on to me like that."

"Well, if I'd been there, he'd now be unable to crawl under the sheets with anyone for a long, long time," he said with a tightening of his lips. "I wish I'd come over just about that time."

At that moment, Krissie came running back to them. "Pony ride," she begged, holding out her arms to Reece.

"Krissie," Deanna admonished. Her daughter was usually bashful around people she had just met, but she seemed instinctively trusting of Reece.

Grinning, he swung Krissie up on his shoulders and pretended to trot, bouncing her up and down. "Ride 'em, cowgirl. Want to race your mother to the house?"

Without waiting for an answer, he darted ahead with Krissie squealing loudly as she rode on his shoulders. Deanna made a valiant effort not to be left too far behind, but they were waiting for her on the front steps when she arrived, puffing.

"Don't say it," Deanna warned him, somewhat breathless.

"Say what?" he asked innocently as he lowered Krissie to the porch.

"That I'm disgracefully out of condition."

"A good run every morning would do you good," he offered diplomatically.

"Not on your life! My mornings are already nightmares with all I have to do."

"Maybe you need a little help." He leaned against the door frame. His grin was openly flirtatious.

She ignored the implied offer. "Do you want to come in and look at some old photos that Mrs. Caruthers brought by?"

He hesitated.

"What's the matter?"

"I don't like looking at old pictures," he said bluntly. "Sometimes they bring back memories that are best forgotten."

"But sometimes they have the opposite effect," she argued. "And bring back good feelings that should be remembered."

She studied his expression. His eyes suddenly seemed shuttered against her. How would he react to all the photos of them standing next to each other? Would he see the adolescent adoration in her eyes as she looked at him? Would he feel again the bond that had been between them? Maybe he didn't want to be reminded of those happy times. *Or were they happy times for him?* She wondered if her memory of him was accurate at all. Maybe she had imagined the affection she had always felt he held for her. She searched his face, seeking some link between the person he had been then and the one he was now.

He responded to her intense scrutiny with a shrug. "Well, okay, why not? Let's take a walk down memory lane."

Krissie bounded into the house ahead of them and headed for the kitchen. Reece followed Deanna into the living room.

She went to the coffee table where she had left the photos. The envelope of pictures was gone, but on the small table was a beautiful heart-shaped box of candy, more expensive than any she had for sale in the store. Embossed printing read "To My Sweetheart." Deanna's skin began to prickle. How did it get there? She had locked the door before they left. Staring at the extravagant gift, her hands clenched tightly at her sides, she knew there was only one answer. *Someone had put it there while she was at the park.*

She swung around as alarm leapt into her eyes. Words caught in her throat as she saw Reece standing in front of the sofa, looking down at the cushions.

"What—?" she gasped. She couldn't believe what she was seeing.

The old photographs were lined up in measured order across the cushions. She stared at them in horror. In every case, a straight pin had been stuck through her head.

Chapter Eleven

Love...hate. Love...hate. The two emotions lashed out at her with the force of a physical assault. Love... Sweet valentine candy. Hate... Sharp pins thrust through her head. Love...hate. Love...hate. The words echoed in her mind like a vicious undercurrent sweeping her along toward destruction. She must have cried out because Krissie came running in from the kitchen.

She grabbed Deanna's legs. "Mommy! Mommy!"

A wave of hysteria poured over Deanna. Her vision blurred. Her chest rose and fell in uneven rhythm.

Reece put a steadying arm around her and held her firmly against his chest. "Easy does it," he soothed and then eased her into a chair.

Krissie promptly climbed into her mother's lap. I have to pull myself together, thought Deanna. I mustn't let Krissie see how frightened I am. Deanna put her cheek against the little girl's face, hugging her tightly. "It's all right, honey," she murmured. "Mommy just had an ugly surprise."

"Are you all right now?" Reece asked, hovering over her. "I'll get you a glass of water."

Deanna closed her eyes. She was in the middle of a horrible nightmare. Someone was deliberately torturing her. None of this could be happening—but it was.

When Reece came back, he handed her the water and then motioned toward the array of photographs. "Are these the ones Mrs. Caruthers brought?"

She nodded. Again, she told herself that the doors had been locked, but someone had been in the house while she and Krissie were at the park. Even as she thrust the suspicion away, it slithered to the front of her mind. *Reece said he'd been by the house earlier.* Meeting her and Krissie on the way home from the park could have been contrived. Had he somehow managed to get in, leave the candy and arranged the photos for her to find?

Reece followed Deanna's stunned gaze to the lavish box of chocolates. With a puzzled expression, he picked it up. "To My Sweetheart" he read aloud. His eyes narrowed. "A gift from someone?"

Deanna looked at him for a long moment before answering. "It wasn't here when I left the house."

"Didn't you lock up before you left?"

"Of course, I did." She took a deep breath to lower the pitch of her voice. "I'm going to call the police. Jump down, Krissie."

The little girl looked enviously at the pretty heart-shaped box. "I like candy. Keep it?" she asked with childish innocence.

"No, darling. This candy isn't for eating."

It could be poisoned.

Deanna's voice was strangely calm when she called the police and reported a break-in.

While they waited for the officers to arrive, Reece continued to stand in front of the sofa and look at the photographs. His expression revealed nothing about his secret thoughts.

When she heard the doorbell, a sinking feeling twisted her insides. Last night it had been the store that had been violated ... and now it was her home.

The same officers, McDowell and Hanks, asked the same questions they had the night before.

How did the intruder get in?

Who had keys to the house? No sign of a broken window or door.

Had anyone been threatening her in any way?

Deanna moistened her dry lips and told them about the unpleasant visit she'd had from Tony DeVargas.

"He's a boyfriend of yours?" the gray-haired officer asked.

"No," she answered emphatically. "Tony's been dating the college girl who lives with me. But today—" She felt a warm flush ease into her cheeks. "Today he came on to me. A neighbor's visit interrupted his advances. He was furious when he left."

"Did he have the box of candy with him?"

"Not that I saw. But I guess he could have come back." She related the incident with the ugly valentine pinned to the door with the butcher knife. "Tony denied doing it, but I'm sure he was lying. It's just the kind of sick joke he'd play. Anyway, he needed a key to open the door that night...and he could have used it again to get in today."

"Where does he live?"

"I don't know. He's a student."

"Well, we can find out from the college. We'll bring him in for questioning." McDowell turned to Reece. "Do you have anything to add?"

Reece shook his dark head. "Afraid not. I didn't see anyone when I came to the door earlier. I rang the bell and when Deanna didn't answer, I took off toward the park."

The officer gave him a measuring look, then he turned to Deanna. "Well, we'll have a little talk with this DeVargas fellow. We'll take the candy and photos. Maybe we'll be lucky and pick up a print or two. Has anyone handled the box except you?"

Reece spoke up. "I did."

"I suppose you handled the pictures, too?"

"No. They're still pinned to the sofa just the way we found them."

"Good." Sergeant McDowell nodded to Hanks to collect them in separate plastic bags.

"I thought you were going to put some surveillance on the house?" Reece asked in a critical tone.

"We've included this address in a routine drive-by," McDowell answered. "But we don't have cause for a twenty-four-hour surveillance." He turned to Deanna. "As I advised you last night, get your house locks changed, Mrs. Donovan, and keep the new keys where other people can't get them."

"I'll do my best. But my college boarder is careless with hers."

"Then warn her about the dangers. I'd say we're dealing with a real weirdo."

After the policemen had gone, Deanna leaned against the door and closed her eyes.

Would the nightmare ever end?

SHE SLEPT BADLY that night and wished a dozen times she hadn't been so stubborn about not letting Reece stay. He had argued that she was being utterly stupid to reject his protection, at least until the locks were changed.

She wasn't afraid he would force himself upon her if he stayed the night. The intimacy they'd shared had been born of mutual desire. Why refuse his offer, she asked herself, chiding the reluctance that kept her from the support he offered. The few hours they'd spent at the Silver Spur were the happiest she'd known. Feelings that she had thought dead forever had been rekindled at his touch. She wanted to be with him with every fiber of her being, and yet she couldn't accept his offer to move into the house.

Why? Was she afraid her own growing feelings for him might blind her to the truth?

What truth?

As she lay rigid in bed, straining to hear every night sound, she tried to find a logical answer for everything that had happened—and failed.

ONLY ONE WEEK till Valentine's Day. When she went into the store the next morning, she was confronted with the shocking vandalism that had sickened her on Saturday night. The vicious, deliberate destruction created an uneasiness that mounted with every sweep of her broom. The teddy bear with its severed head confirmed the influence of a demented mind, and every box of broken pottery she dumped in the trash seemed to represent a hatred that threatened her life. Even when the storeroom was cleared of all the mess, and new locks had been ordered for the store and the house, the uneasiness remained.

Later in the morning, when a United Federal truck drove up, she prayed that it wasn't delivering more expensive pottery—but it was.

Two more boxes.

The uniformed driver looked at her in surprise when she signed for them because her hand was trembling.

"Is something the matter?" he asked.

She shook her head and then asked impulsively, "Do you remember if you've delivered boxes from Southwest Pottery before this week?"

"Gosh, to tell you the truth, I don't pay that much attention to the packages."

"No, I suppose not," she said wearily.

"Sorry."

"It's all right. I just thought I'd ask."

"Maybe I could find out for you," he volunteered. "They keep records of that kind of thing at the office. Might take a little time to check it out, though."

"I'd really appreciate it."

"Sure. No problem." He tipped the brim of his hat and left.

She had to put a stop to the delivery of the expensive giftware. Whatever plans her parents might have had for the expansion of the store, she was in no position to follow through. She prayed that some kind of insurance was in place for the vandalism she had already suffered.

With the invoice in her hand, she went to the telephone and phoned the Southwest Pottery Company in Albuquerque, New Mexico. Her call was transferred several times before she was connected to the correct office and a Mr. Rawlins verified the orders placed by Dee's Candy and Gift Shop.

She explained that she had inherited the store from her parents. "I wish to cancel all back orders," Deanna told him.

"I don't see any back orders. Merchandise has been sent out as orders were received. Let's see. The last one was placed January 24th and—"

"What? January 24th? That's impossible. Any order placed by the owners of the store would have had to be no later than December of last year." She swallowed hard. "That's when my parents were killed."

"I see." He must have heard the tremor in her voice because he said quickly, "Why don't I check our records and get back to you? A computer error could be showing that three orders have been placed since January of this year."

She thanked him and hung up. It couldn't be. There had to be a mistake. A computer foul-up. It happened all the time. People were always getting astronomical bills or fantastic checks that turned out to be mistakes. She shook off a rising apprehension and went to the front of the store to wait on three customers.

When the telephone ring brought her back to her desk, her hands were moist with hot sweat as she lifted the receiver.

Mr. Rawlins informed her that there had been no computer mistake. "I have the order blanks in my hands," he told her. "They are dated January 5, January 15 and January 24 and they are signed by Jim Anderson."

"But that's impossible. My father, Jim Anderson, died on December 29th."

"They were paid for by his credit card number," he insisted.

"But my father's wallet was still in his pocket when his body was found. All his cards and twenty-four dollars in cash were still there."

"May I ask what happened to your father?"

"He was killed during a robbery at the store."

There was a pause. "And money was left in his wallet?"

She closed her eyes as a sharp pain shot through her head. Robbery, that's what the police had said. She had believed their assurance that the same kind of lawlessness went on all the time. She had accepted the rationale that her parents had been victims of a sick society. Now, doubt shot through her head, making her feel as if someone were striking her skull with a hammer.

"I'm sorry, Mrs. Donovan. Under the circumstances, we will be glad to credit your account if you wish to return the merchandise."

Return the merchandise. Boxes filled with broken pottery rested in the trash.

"I'm afraid that won't be possible." Her neutral voice sounded like someone else's as she told him about the vandalism.

"You really are having a turn of bad luck, aren't you?"

"Yes, bad luck," she echoed.

Sounding anxious to conclude their business, he assured her, "I will make certain that no further orders are filled without calling you for authorization, Mrs. Donovan. And if I were you, I would look into insurance coverage provided by the credit card company. Perhaps you can recover your loss."

"Yes. Thank you."

He politely offered to help in any way he could and hung up without the usual banal "Have a nice day."

Deanna stared at the phone for a long moment and then went into the bathroom and took two aspirin.

For the rest of the morning, she waited on customers and spent the quiet periods going through her father's desk. She had only glanced at the contents of the drawers before but now she drew out everything. His signature was all over bills, canceled checks and copies of letters.

She found a pad of order blanks from the Southwest Pottery Company. She could tell that several had been lifted from the gummed tablet.

Signature. Order blanks. What about his credit card number? She couldn't find it listed anywhere in his desk. Leaning back in the chair, she put her fingers against her temples. The card had been found in her father's wallet at the time of his death. No one had taken it. And yet a forger had used it for placing bogus orders.

He only needed the number.

Her blood chilled as she pictured the killer methodically drawing out the card, writing down the number and then putting it back into her dead father's pocket.

Once more, she called the police and reported what she had discovered. They promised someone would get back to her. The phone rang again just as Nellie came in. It was Reece.

"Hi. How about lunch?" he asked. "I know a nice little hole-in-the-wall that serves wonderful tempura shrimp."

"Sorry, I can't. I have to take care of some store business."

"How about tonight? I won't keep you out late. We need to talk. Get some things straightened out."

She was tempted. More than ever she needed to share her confusion with someone. Reece might be able to put together some pieces of the puzzle. He might know— She didn't finish the thought as doubt and suspicion skirted the edges of her mind. *He might know everything.*

No, not Reece. Please, don't let it be Reece, she thought. Her feelings were in a tangle where he was concerned and she was dangerously close to shutting her eyes and giving in to the blind trust that mocked her common sense. The need to be with him almost overrode her good judgment.

"I'm going to be busy tonight," she managed to say. "Perhaps another time," she added rather formally.

THE LOUD CLICK in his ear as she hung up made Reece glower at the phone. He was tempted to call her right back. She'd practically slammed down the receiver. That meant she was tighter than an over-wound spring. One thing was clear. She meant to keep him at a distance. Damn. After everything that had happened, she was still resisting him.

With an angry shove of his chair, he rose to his feet, took the stairs two at a time and stalked out of the bookstore. He was across the street from the bank when Deanna came out and headed down the mall. He stood in the doorway of a busy T-shirt shop across the street and watched her. Her lithe body moved in a graceful rhythm that accentuated her femininity, arms swung easily at her side and tight jeans molded the sweet curves of her hips and legs. Watching her brought a remembrance of that luscious body pressed against his.

He followed her at a discreet distance. She had a date for lunch. He was sure of that. Several cafés on the mall offered outdoor dining and even though February temperatures were on the crisp side, the sidewalk tables were filled with the lunch crowd. A man got up from one of the tables and stepped in front of Deanna as she reached the café. He said something to her, and motioned with his head toward his table. Then he put a possessive arm around her waist and led her to a chair.

All the latent jealousy that Reece had held in check for many years exploded in his head. She had lied to him. She had said her marriage was over. She'd led him to think the feelings she'd had for her ex-husband had died. Now, here she was having lunch with Brad Donovan.

Reece turned away. Fury mingled with despair. He had thought the heartache of the past was over, but once again the girl he had loved since grade school had made a fool of him.

Chapter Twelve

Deanna had been heading for the Sweet Shoppe to talk to Darrel when she passed the outdoor café and heard someone call her name. Brad intercepted her. He gave her his charming people-management smile.

"Hi. I was hoping to run into you. Come on, I have a table. We can talk over lunch."

Her first impulse was to turn on her heels and leave him standing there, but the urge to tell him off got the better of her. She had plenty to say to him.

He put his arm around her waist and led her to the table with a proprietary manner that left her fuming. Reluctant to make a scene, she held back her anger as he gallantly seated her at the small, round table. There was such a satisfied curve to his smile that she wondered if he had been sitting there waiting for her to come by. A more disturbing thought struck her—had he been spying on her?

"Just like old times," he said, leaning toward her. "Remember how we used to stroll down from the campus and have beer and pretzels on the mall? Now, here we are again. Some things never change."

"Neither do some people," she answered shortly as she picked up a menu. She ordered a pastrami sandwich, not a favorite of hers, but food wasn't uppermost in her mind at the moment. She forced herself to sit there and act civilized when in truth she felt like relieving her feelings by throwing something at him.

Brad turned his flirtatious charm on high, chatting easily with the waitress and keeping up a lively monologue that to nearby observers must have marked him as the most entertaining of dining companions. Deanna maintained a rigid silence, some detached part of her looking at him and wondering why she hadn't seen through his egotistical shallowness from the very beginning. He either was ignoring her arctic coolness or was unaware of it, she thought as he talked about the time he'd been spending looking over the campus and reminiscing.

"I've missed you, honey. I haven't been able to quit thinking about how crazy in love we were. Coming back to Boulder made me realize what a special thing we had going between us." He grabbed her hand before she could move it away. "And we haven't lost it. I know we haven't. If you would just—"

"Save it, Brad." She withdrew her hand. "What I felt for you died a long time ago."

"You don't mean that." He actually looked shocked. "How can you turn your back on us ... on our marriage?"

"You made it easy. Now, listen, Brad." She straightened. She'd let him role-play the wounded ex-husband long enough. "I have no intention of letting you back in my life again."

"You need me," he argued. "You've got more than you can handle and you know it. Too many problems. You'll never be able to make the business succeed the way things are going."

Too many problems. Her hand trembled as she picked up her water glass to wash down a piece of sandwich that seemed to grow three sizes in her mouth.

"Dee Dee, it would be a shame if you lost the store because you were too stubborn to let me help."

"What do you know about my ... my problems?"

He hesitated and then said, "Nicki keeps me up-to-date. She's worried about you, honey. And so am I. I guess you know that she's really pushing for us to get back together again. She loves Krissie, our wonderful little daughter."

Deanna leaned toward him, her eyes flashing like a pair of burning matches. "Your little campaign to get to me through Nicki isn't going to work. I'm warning you, Brad. Quit using her. Stay away from Nicki!"

"I guess that's up to Nicki, isn't it?" he countered. "Until she says she doesn't want my company, I'll see that pretty young thing whenever I like."

"Not at *my* house."

He gave her a patient smile. "In some ways, you're such a child, Deanna. You know darn well we should be living in that house together. I'm ready to settle down in Boulder. Why are you so foolish as to try to shut me out? I want to raise my daughter."

"You are to see Krissie by arrangement. And I'll decide when that will be. Don't push me, Brad. I'm warning you. Your docile little Dee Dee has grown a set of long claws."

He was smiling at her rather smugly. "You know I always get what I want, honey. At the moment, I want to see more of my wife and my little girl. It's been hell these last few months without you."

"Save it, Brad. It's too late."

"No, I won't believe that. You still love me. I know you do."

"It's over, Brad." Her eyes locked firmly with his. "Listen to me. I can't deny your parental right to see Krissie. We'll arrange for visitation the way the judge ordered and you can start being the father you never were. But get this straight, Brad. I'll never go back to you. Never."

As he looked into her fixed gaze, his voice suddenly lost its bravado. His handsome face crumpled. "I'm sorry, honey, really sorry."

Sorry? She'd never heard that word on Brad's lips before. Whatever happened was always someone else's fault. Never his. She had never seen him so shaken. He wasn't acting now.

"I don't know why I was so blind. I had everything a man could want, and I blew it. Please, give me a chance. I want to be a good father to Krissie. I want to spend time with my daughter, get to know her."

At one time, the tactic of bringing Krissie into the conversation would have made Deanna feel guilty, but she knew what an indifferent father Brad had been the first three years of their daughter's life. He had used Krissie the way he used everybody else—to get his own way, to stroke his own ego.

"People can change, Dee Dee," he said as if reading her thoughts. "Life is no damn good anymore. I dream about you...reach for you in the night. It's torture. I can't sleep." He grabbed her hand. "There'll never be another woman in my life, Dee Dee. It's you...forever."

His declaration was like an invisible net settling over her, trapping her. A piece of paper that said they were divorced meant nothing to him. That thought brought her to her feet. Her voice betrayed her emotion. "I gave you five years of my life, Brad. Now I have my freedom and I'm going to keep it."

She fled the café and walked along the mall, blinking back hot tears of fury. Her thoughts were like leaves whipped in a devil's wind.

HE KEPT at a discreet distance, but followed close enough to see the defiant lift of her chin as she moved in and out of milling shoppers. He loved the way her hair swung easily on her shoulders as she walked. One summer, she had cut it short in a style no longer than a boy's in the back and he had hated it. She'd only laughed at him when he told her so. Just thinking about the way she'd brushed him aside made the anger build inside him. She never knew how much her cold look could hurt.

Patience, he told himself. Things would soon be different. Only a week until Valentine's Day.

He hoped she would wear red for the celebration.

BRAD HAD UNSETTLED her so badly that Deanna needed a little time to compose herself. She sat down on a mall bench beside a couple of elderly women who were catching their breaths. A weak sun splashed light on brick walks, and shoppers wandered along the mall. Snow still lay upon the flower beds and people were bundled up as usual.

Deanna's stomach tightened in a knot as she went over the conversation with Brad. She'd never seen him so contrite. Was he as shaken as he seemed to be? Lost in her thoughts, she was hardly aware when the two women got up and left and someone else sat down beside her.

When an arm slid behind her on the bench railing, she came out of her reverie with a jerk. Ready to spring to her feet, she gasped in surprise, "Reece."

"I saw you sitting here like you'd lost your last friend. Didn't the lunch date with your ex go well?"

She looked at him in surprise. "How did you know?"

"I saw you. You could have told me Brad was the reason you turned down having lunch with me."

"But I didn't...I mean, that wasn't the reason. We accidentally ran into each other—"

"I doubt that," he countered flatly. "The meeting looked orchestrated to me. At least on his part."

She nodded. "I think you're right. Brad was probably watching for me. I was foolish enough to think that we could talk and get some things straightened out, but I was wrong—oh, so wrong," she said with a catch in her throat. "He's determined to push me into a reconciliation."

Reece tightened his grip on her shoulder. "Hey, don't let the guy spook you. He doesn't have any claims on you anymore."

"He's Krissie's father. He's going to try to get to me through her. He says he's changed, and he wants to be a better father to her. I want to believe him."

"But you don't," he said flatly.

She moistened her dry lips. "I don't know what to think. I've never seen him so...so humble. And shaken up. He worries me."

"Are you ready to admit that he could be the one harassing you? Trying to get you so frightened that you'll turn to him for help? He could be the one responsible for leaving the box of candy at the house and sticking pins in the photos.''

Her lips trembled. "Brad didn't mention the vandalism, but he knows I'm having problems at the store," she admitted.

A glowering expression crept across Reece's face. "Dammit, tell him to get lost. You don't need him around for support. He never took care of you when he had the chance.''

"There's no way I can keep him entirely out of my life. He has legal visitation rights with Krissie. And Nicki's got blinders on where Brad's concerned. He's been using her to keep close tabs on me. There's no way I can forbid him to see Nicki if he wants to. She has some weird notion that we should get back together again and she's ready to do anything he wants to further that end.''

"So what are you going to do?" He lifted a wayward curl drifting forward on her cheek and put it gently behind her ear.

She leaned her head back against his arm and sighed. "I don't know. And I haven't told you the latest development at the store.''

"What's happened now?"

"I got another delivery of pottery this morning, so I called the company to stop any more shipments that my parents had ordered." A bewildered expression crossed her face. "Only they didn't. Order them, I mean. The company said they received all the orders in January. How could that be? My parents couldn't have placed them. I didn't place them. But the orders came in with my father's signature and his credit card number."

"Maybe some salesman decided to increase his commission and placed the forged orders," Reece offered in a reasonable tone. "Your parents could have ordered something else from the guy and he used the signature and credit card number for the bogus orders. I bet the police can track it down."

"I hope so." She began to relax. Reece's matter-of-fact approach to the problem was reassuring. "Anyway, I decided to talk to Darrel, to see if he had any ideas." She smiled. "And that's the reason I couldn't make it for lunch. I was on my way to see him when Brad stopped me."

"Want me to come with you?"

She looked into his concerned face and knew that's what she wanted very much. She wanted to be in his company, to feel his support, and benefit from his calming influence. All of the suspicions, uneasiness and doubts she'd had about him dissipated like frost under a warm sun. "Yes, please."

She slipped her arm through his and remained at his side as they walked along the mall until they reached the Sweet Shoppe.

They found Darrel all aflutter as usual. With Valentine's Day only seven days away, he was preparing an advertising blitz that dwarfed Deanna's tiny newspaper ad. His small office looked like the aftermath of a hurricane. All the chairs were stacked with boxes and he shifted them to his overloaded desk so they could sit down. Deanna remembered the hassles her parents had had with him about the storeroom clutter, which he was supposed to organize and seldom did. Her mother usually ended up putting everything in order. Whenever they came back from a trip after leaving Darrel in charge, she had to spend days straightening up the mess. But, all in all, he had been a good employee. A trusted one.

"I need your help," Deanna began, and was rewarded by a satisfied gleam in his eyes. She explained the situation as succinctly and unemotionally as she could.

He listened, his round eye blinking. "Someone's been ordering merchandise for the store and you don't know who?"

"That's about it," she admitted.

"But why?"

Reece shifted impatiently. "If we knew that, Darrel, we'd know who it was, wouldn't we?"

"Yes, of course, but... well, I mean, it's so bizarre. I haven't the foggiest idea why anyone would do such a thing. Of course, there's no harm done. I mean, you can either return or sell the stuff, can't you?"

"The store was vandalized Saturday night," Deanna told him. "And all the pottery was smashed."

"Smashed?" Darrel echoed as if his brain refused to compute the word.

"Smashed—as in broken to smithereens," Reece snapped. "Someone got in the store and wrecked the storeroom."

Darrel dropped his fat bottom into a chair. "I can't believe it. Another break-in?"

Reece leaned forward and slammed his fist on the desk. "Not a break-in, Darrel. Someone got in with a key. Do you, by any chance, still have a key to Dee's Candy and Gift Shop?"

"You're not suggesting that I—?" He stopped, horrified.

"No, of course not," Deanna said, sending Reece a warning glance. Nothing would be gained by scaring the guy half to death. "Darrel, do you know of anyone who might have had access to my father's signature and credit card number?"

He glared at Reece. "Any business that ever charged something to him. I mean, the credit card system invites scams that are big enough to drive a moving van through." His hands fluttered nervously. "Everybody knows that. Really, Deanna, I find this whole conversation very distasteful." His voice took on a whining edge. "I was a loyal employee of your parents for ten years. I don't appreciate your coming in here and—and, well, practically accusing me of doing such terrible things."

"I'm not accusing you of anything, Darrel. I thought you might be able to offer a reason that someone would want to order pottery for the store and then destroy it."

"Well, I can't."

"Maybe it's someone who wants to see Dee's store go into bankruptcy," suggested Reece pointedly.

"There you go again," Darrel said with a reproachful glare. "Really, I mean, I'd have nothing to gain by indulging in such lawlessness. All the breakage will be covered by the insurance. You're lucky a credit card was used, Deanna. No financial loss." He turned to Reece. "I mean, really, how would I benefit in the least?"

"If Deanna decided that the harassment was too great and closed her store, yours would be the only one left on the mall. You would have eliminated your competition."

"Nonsense." Darrel fixed his round, guileless eyes on Deanna and gave her his widest smile. "You know I only wish you the best, Deanna, dear."

With a flourish, he handed her a chocolate rose with a tag that read "Be My Valentine."

Chapter Thirteen

"I never liked that guy," Reece mumbled as they walked back to her store.

"I'd say that was pretty obvious," Deanna answered wryly. "You were less than subtle when it came to pointing a finger at him. Darrel's not at the top of my list of likable people, either, but it's ridiculous to think he'd spend his time ordering and destroying stock for my store."

"Not so ridiculous if you get upset enough to eliminate his competition. I bet he's already made some suggestions about merging or buying you out."

She looked at him in surprise. "How did you know? As a matter of fact, that's exactly what he suggested."

"And what did you say?"

"What do you think?" She jutted out her chin.

He frowned. "Sounds as if you threw down a gauntlet. Darrel could have decided to force the matter. If the harassment keeps up, you might change your mind about cooperating with him.''

She shook her head and impulsively slipped her arm through his. The brush of his body against hers as they walked felt warm and comforting. He smiled as if he was also aware of the teasing delight of walking closely together. They looked like one of the many couples strolling arm in arm along the mall, idly window-shopping and chatting. Sharing her problems with him came easily. During those growing-up years, she'd been able to talk to him about almost everything. The companionship they'd shared had been very special and even though they both had changed since those days, the old habit of confiding in him quickly surfaced.

''I don't know what's going on, but I don't think Darrel's at the bottom of it.''

''Who else could it be?'' Reece insisted. ''He would know how to use the order blanks and credit card number. All these years, he's seen your father's signature enough to forge it. If he can shake you up enough, you may decide to turn over the business to him.''

''I'm not giving up the store to Darrel. Nor to anyone else,'' she added as she remembered Brad's insistence that the house and store should be shared with him. When they were married, she had given in to him just to have peace of mind. Never again! She drew in a deep breath and leveled her gaze at Reece.

"It will take more than a bunch of broken pottery to make me turn heel and run."

Instead of a smile, she saw the worry lines around his eyes deepen. "That's what I'm afraid of."

SHE DIDN'T HAVE time to think about anything but selling candy and valentine gifts. She was grateful for the constant clang of the cash register. At about four o'clock, the director of Krissie's day-care called. Deanna's heart immediately leapt into her throat when the woman identified herself.

"This is Miss Davenport at Mother Goose Daycare. I'm sorry to bother you, but we have a little problem here. According to Krissie's records, no one is authorized to pick her up from the center except you. Is that correct?"

"Yes." Her mouth was dry.

"I just wanted to check. Mr. Donovan is here and Krissie seems eager enough to go with him, but—"

"No. She's to go home in the van as usual. Her father only has visitation rights for two weekends a month. Don't let him take her."

"We won't, Mrs. Donovan. You can depend upon us to follow your instructions."

"Thank you." Deanna hung up and stared at the phone, unable to still the quivers in her chest. *What if Brad decided to take Krissie without anyone's permission?* Child-napping was common enough with fathers who wanted custody of their children. No, her ex-husband wasn't like that, she tried to reassure herself. The Bradley Donovan she knew had never shown any possessive tendencies toward his child.

She rushed home after work and was relieved to find Krissie happily playing, putting together a wooden puzzle with her baby-sitter.

"Rough day?" Nicki asked, eyeing Deanna's anxious face.

She just nodded. At the moment, she didn't feel like sharing anything about Brad with Nicki.

THE NEXT FEW DAYS passed swiftly and uneventfully. On Wednesday, the United Federal driver stopped to tell her he'd gotten the information she wanted.

"I made the first delivery from that company a week ago, Tuesday."

"Nothing from Southwest Pottery Company before that?"

"Nope. Here's a copy of the shipping invoices."

Deanna studied them eagerly but they added nothing new. The dates were the same ones that the company had given her. Nothing indicated who had ordered the merchandise or why.

"Does that help?" he asked eagerly.

"Yes, it does," she lied. She thanked him for his trouble and he left, whistling, as if she'd convinced him that he'd done a good deed.

For the rest of the week, Deanna had little time to think about anything but the immediate demands of store and home. The police had talked to Tony, and he had retaliated by cornering Nicki on campus and making a scene. Nicki didn't repeat the whole conversation but related enough for Deanna to know that he had told the police that she was a vicious, sex-starved divorcée who had forced him to break up with Nicki because she couldn't bear to see him paying attention to her college boarder.

"He also told them you're a neurotic woman who was capable of creating ugly incidents just to get attention. In fact, he's sure that you stuck that repulsive valentine on your own door."

Deanna blanched.

"I told him to crawl back under his rock," Nicki declared with a toss of her blond hair.

No wonder Sergeant McDowell looked at her with undisguised skepticism when he questioned her again about the vandalism, thought Deanna, remembering the policeman's second visit to the store.

"Are you sure you didn't order the pottery yourself, Mrs. Donovan? Maybe you forgot . . . ?"

"Forgot that my father was dead when I forged his name and used his credit card?" she snapped. Then she took a deep breath and said in an even tone, "I haven't placed any orders since I took over the store. The pottery shipments were completely unexpected. Someone else ordered them."

"For what reason? If the person who ordered the pottery was the same one who destroyed it, there has to be an motive other than vandalism. There were plenty of other things in the store that could have been destroyed if that was the only object." His heavy eyebrows matted over the high bridge of his nose and there was an accusing edge to his voice. "The destruction was very selective. I know that you have been put through an emotional wringer, Mrs. Donovan, with the tragic death of your parents, your divorce and the responsibility of taking over a business. A heavy load. It's understandable that you might—"

"I did *not* place the orders. I did *not* break the pottery." She met his eyes without blinking. "Someone is doing these things to me. And it is your job to find out who before..." Her voice broke.

"Before what, Mrs. Donovan?"

"Before he gets tired of fun and games and does something horrible."

"Nothing horrible is going to happen," he reassured her, but he gave her a long look before he stuck his pencil and notebook back in his pocket. "We located your ex-husband and had a long talk with him. He's rented a condo in the Foothills addition, and I understand he's signed a contract with the Boulder school district to finish out the year for a coach who had to take a leave of absence."

"That's news to me," Deanna said with a sinking feeling. So Brad was here to stay. That meant he'd want visitation rights and there was nothing she could do about it.

"He spoke very highly of you, Mrs. Donovan. Even expressed the hope that there might be a reconciliation. He was aware that you are under a great deal of pressure."

And Brad's part of it, she thought silently.

"We dusted those photographs for prints."

"Did you find any?"

"Dozens." He snorted. "Half the people in Boulder must have handled those prints at some time or other."

"Mrs. Caruthers probably showed them around a lot," Deanna agreed. "She was proud of her kids and was always pointing a camera at anyone who would stand still a minute."

"We only found two sets of prints on the candy box. Yours and Ryndell's." He watched her face. When she didn't respond, he said, "Well, be sure and call us if anything else happens."

His words hung in the air like an insidious vapor. After he'd gone, she said aloud, "Dear God, let this be the end of it."

As if in answer, the telephone rang. It was her ex-husband wanting to make arrangements to have Krissie overnight on Saturday. "I know you won't let me pick her up at day-care. Miss Davenport made that clear enough. So I want her for the weekend. You can't go against the court ruling, Dee."

She closed her eyes. *No, you can't have her.*

"Are you listening to me? She's my daughter and I intend to see her."

Deanna took herself in hand and asked calmly, "Why not just for the day? You know how Krissie's asthma sometimes flares up at night."

"The judge said I could have her for two weekends a month. Remember? Well, I have this nice place now and a job and I want to exercise my visitation rights. I thought I'd take her to the Denver zoo on Saturday afternoon. If you'd like to come along, too—?" The invitation hung in the air.

Damn him! If she went with them, it would be a retreat from the independence the divorce had given her. Pulling up marital roots had been painful. She wasn't about to risk putting them down again. There wasn't anything she could do but let him take Krissie. She, however, declined his invitation to join them.

They made arrangements for him to pick Krissie up on Saturday morning and bring her back on Sunday afternoon. The little girl seemed excited by the new adventure, and Deanna tried to hide the queasy feeling in her stomach as she packed an overnight bag for her daughter.

"I'm going to be gone this weekend, too," Nicki told Deanna. "A bunch of us are going up to a ski lodge at Beaver Creek. There's this guy." Her eyes sparkled. "I met him in my math class. He says the slopes have new powder and the skiing is great. I'm not much on skis, but he said he'd teach me." She giggled.

"Sounds like fun."

"You'll be all right here alone, won't you?"

"Of course," Deanna assured her while an inner voice mocked the confidence in her voice. "I've got a dozen things that need doing around the house. I want to get the front bedroom changed into a sitting room. And I—"

"Do you have a Saturday date with Reece?" Nicki cut in.

She shook her head.

Nicki nodded in approval. "Wise decision."

Deanna didn't say that Reece hadn't asked her. In fact, she hadn't seen nor heard from him for a couple of days. Several times she'd been tempted to stop by the bookstore but had resisted. He'd been in her thoughts a lot more than she'd wanted to admit, and she'd caught herself daydreaming about what fun it would be to go dancing with him again. When she remembered the explosive warmth of his lips on hers, she gave herself a mental shake. *Cool it, girl. You're just good friends, remember?*

Brad picked up Krissie at the store at ten o'clock. He came in with a big red heart-shaped lollipop in his hand. Krissie was delighted and threw herself into his arms.

"Sorry to be patronizing the competition," he told Deanna. "I passed Darrel's store and when I told him I was picking up my little girl, he insisted on selling me the candy."

"If you load her up with sweets, she's going to get sick," Deanna warned. Her maternal instincts fired

on all levels and she spent the next ten minutes going over a list of "dos" and "don'ts."

Brad stuffed the list into his pocket. "We're not
taking off for Siberia, you know. And give me some
credit, Dee Dee. I know how to take care of my
daughter."

Since when? Deanna thought. Tears filled up the
corner of her eyes as she watched them walk hand in
hand out the door. Krissie turned at the last minute
and waved to her. Then she gave her lollipop a lick
and said something to Brad that made him laugh.

Deanna fought an impulse to run and grab her
child. She felt as if her whole world had just walked
out the door. A cry built in her chest and her lower
lip quivered. She shouldn't have let Krissie go. Why
had she let Brad take her?

Because you had no choice, she told herself. And
she had to admit that was true. The law gave him the
right to see his child.

Chapter Fourteen

Reece came into the store at closing time. "I was hoping to catch you before you left. Any chance of buying you a beer, dinner, or all of the above?"

Deanna was a little piqued that he'd waited until the last minute to ask for a date. She was tempted to turn him down flat, but the prospect of going home to an empty house won out. "I might be persuaded," she conceded with a guarded smile.

"Good. I drove above the speed limit all the way from Colorado Springs."

"You've been away?"

"Didn't Nicki give you my message? I had to cover an estate auction for Dad in the Springs. Picked up a good secondhand library, too. Beautiful old gold leaf volumes and leather-bound classics. Unfortunately, the sale went on for two days and the library contents were the last items offered today."

"I guess I didn't see the note," Deanna hedged, knowing that Nicki hadn't written down the message. "Give me a minute to lock up. Nellie left a couple of minutes ago. We're practically sold out of our valentine stock. With Valentine's Day only two days away, there isn't much time to clear everything out. I was tempted to stay open later tonight since it's Saturday and both Krissie and Nicki are away, but I decided I've had enough of the store."

"Wait a minute. Where's Krissie? In the hospital? Did she have another attack?"

"No, thank heavens. Her father took her for the weekend. Brad's decided to exercise his visitation rights." Deanna tried to keep her lower lip from trembling. "He'd better take damn good care of her."

He lifted her chin with his fingertips. "Come on, Dee Dee. Quit worrying. You know you need a break. Enjoy the freedom from motherhood for one night. Now, where would you like to go for dinner. The Silver Spur?"

She shook her head. "I think I'd prefer something less . . . energetic."

"Perhaps some romantic place? With candlelight and wine?"

She smiled at the hopeful lilt of his voice. And suddenly she knew that's exactly what she wanted. "You have some place in mind?"

He grinned. "I do, indeed. The Powderhorn. About five miles up Boulder Canyon. A quiet little place with a huge stone fireplace, knotty-pine walls and good food served with no hustle and bustle."

"Are you sure we should go out of town? The weatherman says a storm is moving in."

"You mean we might get snowbound together? What a catastrophe!" He slipped his arm through hers. "Let's chance it."

Deanna laughed with him. "You're on."

Soft snowflakes settled on their faces as they left the store. Reece had borrowed his father's new car. A light dusting of snow covered the windshield and the two-lane highway winding between high mountain cliffs west of town. Night shadows and dancing snow outside the windows created a closeted feeling in the car, shutting out the world. Deanna found herself relaxing. Her breath became slow and easy. Tension eased from her body.

Reece glanced at her profile as they pulled into a clearing in front of a modest two-story log building. "Hungry?"

"Famished."

He helped her out of the car, and for a moment let his hands rest gently on her arms. As they stood there in the falling snow, ice-blue shadows touched their faces and he kissed away the moist flakes caught on her long lashes. She leaned into him as his mouth found her lips. The wind's chill upon her face was lost in a heat wave of desire sluicing through her body. Only the sound of their quickened breathing broke the stillness of the night. Snow swirling around them went unheeded until he reluctantly lifted his lips from hers and put an arm around her waist as they went into the restaurant.

The snowy night had discouraged other patrons and they practically had the place to themselves. The food was as good as Reece had promised. Their date at the Silver Spur had not been conducive to conversation, because the music and noise level had been too high. In the quiet, warm atmosphere of the secluded restaurant, she found him to be an entertaining dinner companion. He had traveled enough to talk about culinary differences in various countries, and shared some anecdotes about learning to eat with his fingers from community dishes while in Saudi Arabia.

As they lingered over coffee, she asked, "Have you decided what you're going to do next?"

He shook his head. "I've been letting things slide." His face darkened as he began to talk about himself and the battle for life he'd almost lost in a foreign hospital. A fierceness radiated from him that she had never seen before. She listened in horror to the details of the disease that had ravaged his body, and felt overwhelmed at the desolation he'd experienced as his life slipped away from him.

"I kept thinking that I'd let all those years go by without telling you how much I loved you." His eyes were dark, gray pools as he searched her face. "Didn't you know I was waiting for you to grow up, Dee Dee?"

She shook her head regretfully. "No, I didn't. I thought you saw me as a pesky neighborhood kid. After all, you were older, a man of the world. Four years is a big difference during the teen years. I used to dream that we were the same age. Looking at those photos, anyone can tell I had a bad case of puppy love."

"I knew something was developing between us. All those years, I carefully bided my time. I watched you develop from a delightful young girl into a captivating woman. I always believed that when you were ready to make a commitment, you would turn to me. But when that time came, I watched you slip away from me. And I did nothing—nothing."

"It was my fault." She sighed. "I shut you out when I met Brad."

He raised her hand and kissed it softly. "Telling you how much I loved you became an obsession with me as I lay helpless in that hospital bed. I'd wake up in the night, my body bathed in sweat, and I'd call out your name. In my feverish dreams, you were there with me." He took her hand and held it tightly. "In a strange way, you kept me alive."

She blinked against the tears threatening to fill her eyes. The intensity of his passion swept her into dangerous emotional waters. More than anything, she wanted to claim the love that had always been there for her. But too many things had happened. She wasn't the same person she had been before making the mistake of marrying Brad. Now she was wary of her feelings. Afraid to trust herself. Afraid to trust Reece.

"I'm sorry," he said quickly, withdrawing his hand as she searched for words. "I didn't mean to go on like that."

"I'm glad you shared that with me. I never dreamed that I had become so important to you."

"Well, now you know. I really didn't mean to lay all that on you. As they say, the past is history." His eyes grew tender as he looked at her. "I'd best get you home."

The storm had worsened. Waves of falling snow limited visibility, and driving down the icy highway demanded all of Reece's attention. The car slid dangerously on the curves, and the snow tires had trouble gripping the road on the steep inclines. Deanna drew a breath of relief when they finally pulled up in front of her house.

She bent her head against the flying snow as they walked up the sidewalk. She thought she glimpsed faint tracks in the accumulation upon the sidewalk. The wind whirled snow in front of her face and across the ground. She looked again and the tracks had disappeared.

As Reece unlocked the door, nothing but windswept snow scurried across the boards of the porch and steps. She saw no footprints but their own.

Had she been mistaken?

He guided her inside, and she sent a searching look around the foyer and up the stairs. Everything seemed to be as she'd left it. He helped her out of her coat but only unbuttoned his jacket.

"What's the matter?" he asked as he brushed snowflakes from her long lashes.

She swallowed hard. "Nothing."

His eyes narrowed. "You're frightened."

"No, not really. It's just that...well, I thought I saw footprints in the snow leading up to the house. As if someone had been here in the last few minutes. After all that's happened—"

"Stay here. I'll take a look around."

She wandered into the downstairs rooms as he went quickly through the house, upstairs and down. When he'd finished, he gave her a reassuring smile. "All safe and secure."

She felt utterly ridiculous. The footprints must have been an illusion of shadows on the snow. Before she could make some light remark, the telephone rang.

She jumped. Her mouth was instantly dry as she bounded for the hall phone.

Her hello was strained.

"Hi. It's Brad."

"What's wrong?" she gasped. Her hand clenched the phone. "What's happened to Krissie?"

"Not a thing. Hey, relax, will you? I just wanted to report that she's snug in bed. Sleeping peacefully with a new stuffed monkey clutched in her arms. What a great kid." He paused. "You've done a good job with her, Dee Dee."

Relief poured over her. She didn't know what to say. It wasn't like Brad to be humble. "I'm glad you had a good time," she managed to say.

"Listen, honey. I know our marriage wasn't the greatest and it's no use pretending that it was, but I've learned some things the hard way. Are you listening to me?"

"Brad—"

"Please, just listen. Maybe I'll never be the best father in the world. But I want to do right by Krissie. She means a lot to me. If it's really over between us—"

"It is over, Brad. And you can't use Krissie to change things."

"Well, you can't blame me for trying," he countered. "Anyway, I've got a job now and my life is getting back on track."

"I know and I'm glad."

"I called earlier but you were out."

"Yes," she said, without elaborating. She wasn't going to make the mistake of sharing any of her personal life with him. She was going to guard her independence. It had been too dearly bought.

"You're not talking, huh?" He had picked up on her silence. "I suppose that Ryndell fellow Nicki's been telling me about is hanging around?"

"That's none of your concern, Brad."

"Okay, okay. Don't get your dander up."

"I'll plan on seeing you tomorrow afternoon. Early. Kiss Krissie for me. Good night."

She put the receiver back in its cradle. "Krissie's fine," she told Reece.

"Couldn't help overhearing," he said, making no bones about having sat down on the bottom step and listening to her end of the conversation.

"Sounds like he was giving you the third degree."

"Not like he used to. Maybe he's growing up. Anyway, I think he's backing off. It sounds as if Krissie has become very important to him."

"Maybe he's making a calculated maneuver?"

She shook her head. "I don't think so. I'm pretty sure that he accepts the finality of the divorce decree."

"Well, that's good news to me. How about offering me something warm before you send me out in the cold?"

"What did you have in mind?" she asked with a teasing tilt of her head as she looked up at him. "Coffee? Brandy?"

"Is that the best you can do?" He touched wayward curls clinging to her cheeks, and his fingertips trailed over the sweet planes of her face.

"Maybe not." She slipped her hands under the open jacket. For a long moment, she pressed her head against his chest, feeling the long, warm length of his body as she circled his waist tightly. "How's that?"

He chuckled. "It's a start."

She didn't know when the decision was made. At some point, he left his jacket on the newel post and they walked up the stairs to her room.

There was no constraint between them as they lay together. Reece was the gentle lover she had expected him to be. Every touch, every kiss and whisper was part of a building intimacy, unhurried and tantalizing. His hands played tenderly over her soft feminine curves as he molded her body to his. He breathed endearments as lyrical as poetry and expanded her senses to bewildering heights. She was fulfilled as she had never been before, and at the same time frightened by the incredible passion that exploded between them.

She lay awake in his arms long after his heavy breathing told her that he was asleep. It was going to be all right, she told herself. No second thoughts or doubts. This was the man she should have married. Fate had been kind to give them a second chance. She let all her worries float away. For the first time since the death of her parents, she slept soundly.

She awoke once in the night just as he was crawling back into bed.

"Sorry. I didn't mean to wake you." He hugged her close and they fell asleep again.

Since it was Sunday, she hadn't set the alarm. When she awoke the next morning, she heard water running in her adjoining bathroom.

With a broad yawn, she threw on a terry cloth robe and ambled down the hall to the large central bathroom. As she passed Krissie's room, she stopped.

The door was closed.

In all the weeks they'd been in the house, that door had never been closed. She always had left it open so she could hear Krissie if she called.

Her hand was shaking as she turned the doorknob and flung the door open.

She stared in shock, her heart racing madly. It couldn't be!

Every piece of furniture had been moved. The bed and dresser and chest of drawers and rocking chair and bookcase—everything!

The bedroom had been arranged exactly the way it had been when she was a young girl growing up in the house.

Chapter Fifteen

Deanna closed the door and walked back to her room. The shower was still running. She stood in the middle of the floor, hugging herself as tremors rippled up her spine. She stared at the rumpled bed, remembering how she had awakened during the night when Reece crawled back under the covers. She had just assumed he'd gone to the bathroom. Gathering some clothes, she went back to the central bathroom, dressed and went downstairs. In the kitchen, she collapsed into a chair and put her head in her hands. What was she going to do?

Her emotions had blinded her. All the signs had been there and she had ignored them. Her frayed nerves had made her vulnerable to Reece's declarations of love and protection. Now, she knew the truth. He had fixated on the past. In some macabre way, he was trying to recover it. He believed that his love for her had kept him alive and undoubtedly wanted everything to be as it had been before—even to the point of rearranging the furniture to the way it had been when they were growing up.

She shivered as a cold prickling crept over her skin. While she'd slept contentedly, he had been acting out a psychotic compulsion. The teddy bear! He'd been the one to put the stuffed toy in the rocking chair where she had always set Winnie the Pooh.

When they were teens, he had been in and out of their house constantly. He had listened to records in her room, put up a new poster he'd bought for her, and during her sophomore year in high school, he'd come over every night one semester to tutor her when she was flunking chemistry. He knew where everything belonged.

She pressed her fingertips against her aching head, trying to drive out the horrid truth. While she had been at the hospital, he had gained entrance to the house, and then just pretended to arrive after she got home. The same with the box of candy and mutilated photos. He was sick, sick, sick.

What was she going to do?

She heard his footsteps on the stairs and quickly got to her feet. She grabbed the coffeepot and began filling it with water. *Act natural,* she told herself. No telling what he would do if she confronted him. Alone in the house with him was no time to challenge his behavior. Every move she made might trigger the hate that was an intricate part of his love.

"Well, good morning, lovely lady. Did you sleep well?" he asked, coming up behind her and slipping his arms around her waist. He nuzzled her neck, letting his lips taste the soft curve below her ear. His hair was damp from his shower and as the dark strands touched her cheek, she made a pretense of drawing away as if it tickled.

She forced a light laugh. "I slept fine. How about you?" She searched his relaxed, smiling face. A mask, she thought. His eyes were clear, soft and caressing. If she hadn't seen Krissie's room, she would have gone into his arms. She turned away quickly and began taking things out of the refrigerator. She wanted him to leave *now*.

He leaned against the counter so that she had to pass him as she went from refrigerator to stove. She avoided eye contact with him. He stood there watching silently as she moved stiffly about the kitchen.

After a moment, he asked quietly, "What's the matter? Why the icicles?"

She'd have to stick to the truth as much as possible. He knew her too well. "I'm having second thoughts, I guess."

"The morning-after conscience?"

Guilt wasn't anywhere close to the upheaval of emotions that she felt, but she nodded.

"What's there to feeling guilty about? Two people in love spent a wonderful night together. It isn't as if we just met each other," he said with a wry smile.

Her mouth went dry. "I guess I'm just not ready for another commitment. How do you like your eggs?"

"The way your hands are trembling, I think you'd better scramble them." He reached out and took the carton from her. "Now, what's this all about, love?"

"I told you. I'm—I'm not comfortable with what happened. I need time...to think things through. Please, try to understand."

"Were you pretending last night?"

"No, of course not."

His eyes narrowed. "Don't play games with me, Dee Dee. I don't have the patience I used to." His gray eyes were suddenly like iced pewter, bleached of all blue tint.

She moved beyond his reach, picked up the coffeepot and held it in front of her protectively. *You're sick, Reece. And I don't know how to help you.*

As if he read her thoughts, his sensitive mouth grew hard. The air between them was charged like summer lightning. A legion of expressions crossed his face, all of them frightening.

At that moment the phone rang.

Deanna quickly reached for the wall phone, lifting the receiver with relief. She didn't bother to hide her eagerness to accept the interruption as she said hello.

"Hi, Dee. You won't believe who this is," said a merry voice. "Ellen. I'm in town for a few days. How are you?"

"Fine. How nice to hear from you." She kept her back to Reece as she talked. She didn't want him to see the panic in her eyes.

"Mom told me you've moved back with your little girl. I'm sorry things didn't work out with you and Brad. How about me dropping by some time with my two little ones? You and I have a lot of catching up to do."

"That would be great, Ellen. How about . . . how about this morning? I've a fresh pot of coffee all made."

"Are you sure? Kind of short notice."

"No, it'll be fine. See you in a little while."

Deanna hung up, took a deep breath and turned around. "That was—"

The kitchen was empty. She heard the front door slam.

Reece! For an insane moment, she had the urge to run after him. Then she recovered herself. Pretending that everything was normal between them was impossible.

She paced the kitchen. She was suspended in a living nightmare. What now? Call Sergeant Mc-Dowell? Tell him that while she'd slept, her lover had left her bed and moved all the furniture in her girlhood bedroom?

Reece . . . Reece. She wiped tears threatening to spill down her cheeks. Whatever she did was going to cause him more pain. Once she reported him, the police would bring him in for questioning. He'd be immediately caught in an indifferent legal system that could crush him forever. No telling how long it would be before he got the help he needed. There had to be another way.

He'd been seeing Dr. Owens, the same physician who had treated them both since childhood, handling their physicals and inoculations for school. According to Reece, the doctor had given him a clean bill of health. But what about his mind? Dr. Owens was a medical doctor and not a psychiatrist, but he'd know what to do. Yes, she'd tell him about Reece. Between them, they could decide the best way to handle his psychotic illness.

Since it was Sunday, she'd have to wait until the next day to call him. She drew in a deep breath and let it out slowly. For the first time since she'd opened Krissie's bedroom door, she felt in charge of the situation. Dr. Owens would know how to get Reece into therapy. Until then, no one need know about the bizarre moving of the furniture.

Ellen arrived a short time later with her two little boys. Deanna was in no mood for a "remember when" session, but Ellen was just the way she'd always been, outgoing, eager to catch up on what had been happening in their lives since they parted as girlhood friends. Deanna had to force herself to contribute to the conversation.

"It seems like yesterday, doesn't it?" Ellen continued.

Deanna nodded, thinking, *No, it was a lifetime ago.*

Ellen's round face wore a broad smile as she talked about the neighborhood parties they used to have. "We had some good times, didn't we? Mom said she brought you some old photos."

"Yes." She hoped Ellen wouldn't ask to see them. She didn't want her to know that the police had taken them. At the moment, she wasn't up to sharing with anyone all the frightening things that had been happening to her.

"I guess my mom's pretty lonely now that we kids have all moved out," Ellen mused. "I left first, then Benny, and then Richard. And now I've got two rambunctious little boys who are every bit as pesky as my brothers were. I'm hoping that next time I'll have a girl. That's what I want. Two girls and two boys. You know, to even things out. Of course, one child gets more attention," she added as if suddenly remembering that Deanna's divorce had left her with a single child. "Anyway, Dee, you'll marry again. Remember how you used to shuffle your boyfriends so you could date two of them on Saturday, going bike-riding with one guy in the afternoon and taking in a movie with another one at night?" She laughed. "And then there was Reece—"

It was all Deanna could do to keep her expression neutral.

"I always thought that you two... Well, you know what I mean. Even with the age difference, you made a neat couple. Reece was pretty much your shadow when we were growing up. And you had that heavy crush on him when we were in high school, remember?''

"Yes, I remember."

"I guess he was your first love. You always got a dreamy look on your face when Reece was around. I never thought it would happen to me, until I met Homer. Oh, Dee, he's the most..." Ellen was like her mother when it came to monologues, and for once Deanna was glad she didn't have to make conversation.

Ellen's two little boys were all over the house. Their mother yelled at them to quit running, to quit fighting and to quit bringing Krissie's toys down from upstairs, but they ignored her the same way her younger brothers had ignored Mrs. Caruthers. Deanna wondered how Ellen's Homer fit into the rowdy family.

When they were ready to leave, Ellen insisted on gathering up all the toys and taking them upstairs to Krissie's bedroom.

"Oh, how nice!" she exclaimed. "You gave her your old room. And you've left everything exactly the same."

Deanna knew that all color drained from her face, but Ellen didn't seem to notice.

"Gosh, when I walked in here, I felt time slipping backward. Things sure don't change much."

Just people, Deanna thought. The sick feeling returned to her stomach.

Ellen and her little hooligans left before Brad arrived with Krissie. Her daughter had a chocolate grin on her face and was loaded down with zoo souvenirs. Brad looked a little bit like a kid himself. His pants were wrinkled, and his shirt had dribbles of mustard down the front. Playing the good daddy seemed to agree with him. She just hoped he kept it up when parenting wasn't all fun and games. Whether or not she could depend upon him when she needed strong support remained to be seen. For the moment, she was relieved that he had backed off from pushing her for a reconciliation.

"I'd like to have the kid again in a couple of weeks," he told her as he started to leave.

"Call me then and we'll set it up." Her eyes met his in an unspoken message: *I don't want to see you until then.* Her steady eye contact must have made him change his mind about using his people-management charm on her. He nodded and left without saying anything personal.

She had her hands full getting Krissie to settle down and take her nap.

"You moved my bed. Can't see Mother Goose," she wailed, turning her head to try to see her favorite poster.

"We'll move everything back the old way when Nicki comes home," Deanna promised.

"My toys?" she whined, looking at the stuffed animals Ellen had just tossed into a basket.

Deanna explained that she'd had company while Krissie was gone and that two little boys had played with her toys. Krissie set her face in a pugnacious frown. "Don't like boys."

Deanna wasn't in the mood to argue with that.

The afternoon crept by. The weather was gray and dreary with clouds hanging low and snow continuing to fall sporadically. Sometimes the white flakes were as thick as feathers shaken from a pillow. As the wind quickened, it blew them into mounded drifts against fences and shrubs.

Deanna found herself stopping in the middle of a weekend chore to stare blankly into space. She tried to keep her thoughts focused on something besides the heartache that Reece had caused. Maybe she should have handled things differently that morning. She was worried that he might come back or telephone. She didn't want to see him again until Dr. Owens had talked with him.

Her thoughts were as heavy as the lowering storm clouds. When Krissie got up from her nap, she was fussy and difficult to handle. Deanna sighed. Being shuffled back and forth between her parents was going to demand some adjustment from her daughter. Deanna hoped Krissie wasn't going to be this upset after every visit with Brad.

He stood in the shadows of a tall evergreen tree just inside the alley gate and stared at the back of the house. Falling snow whipped around him as bright light through a kitchen window spilled out upon a blue-tinted snowbank. The warm glow drew him closer and closer to the house. He stopped and pressed against the trunk of a tree. He could see her and the child sitting at the kitchen table. It was a scene that made him angry. He should be inside with her, laughing, eating, touching hands and brushing his leg against hers under the table. Instead, he was out in the cold. Shut out and scorned.

Anger and resentment brought a hot flush to his face. An urgency to show her that he couldn't be shoved aside and forgotten swept over him. Right this minute, he could go into the house if he wanted to. He had waited long enough!

He took one step toward the house and then stopped. No, it had to be done right. He forced himself to turn away and leave by the back gate. His cold lips curved with a promise. Tomorrow. Valentine's Day. The waiting would be over.

WHEN EVENING CAME, Deanna was physically tired but still nervously charged up. She knew that the next day would be an exhausting one at the store.

Nicki came home about dusk, happy and tired from a weekend of skiing. "What's been going on with you?"

Deanna took her upstairs and showed her Krissie's room.

"Hey, you moved everything around." Nicki frowned. "How'd you do it all by yourself? Some of this stuff is pretty heavy."

"Reece spent the night here last night," Deanna told her as unemotionally as she could. "Some time in the middle of the night, he got up and moved the furniture." She swallowed hard. "He put everything back the way it was years ago."

"Deanna, what a creep! I knew it. I never liked the look in his eyes. I told you, didn't I? Now this proves it. He's a kook."

"He's not a kook!" Her frayed nerves snapped. "He was very ill for a long time overseas. He almost died. The horrible experience left its mark. For some reason, he's fixated on the past. He needs professional help."

"You can say that again. So he's the one doing all the crazy stuff. He must have gotten hold of your keys the minute we had the locks changed. And you thought it was Tony," she said in an accusing tone. "Well, thank heavens, now we know. What are you going to do?"

Deanna told her about her decision to talk to Dr. Owens.

"I think you should call the police. Now. Tonight."

"No, I can't do that to Reece."

"Why not?" Nicki's eyes rounded. "You're not in love with the guy, are you?"

Deanna turned away without meeting her eyes or answering. "Will you help me put things back the way they were?"

"Sure, but…but you should do something to stop this guy."

"Tomorrow will be soon enough."

Chapter Sixteen

Deanna spent a wretched night. Unable to suppress the memory of Reece's warm body next to hers, she lay stiff and chilled in her bed, filled with new loneliness. Making love with Reece had held out a promise that life could be exciting and fulfilling again. She had reached for this new hope only to be betrayed. She had let down her guard, allowed her feelings to cloud her judgment. Without the chilling incident with the bedroom furniture, no telling how long it would have been before some other bizarre happening would have brought her to her senses.

As the hours ticked slowly by, she firmed her decision to tell the doctor first, and then the police. No matter what her feelings for him might be, she had to protect herself and Krissie.

THE MORNING RUSH was worse than usual. Krissie started crying because they couldn't find the box of valentines Deanna had bought for her to take to school.

"Want valentines," she wailed. "Have to put them into mailbox for the party."

"We'll find them. Where did you have them last?" Krissie didn't remember.

Deanna had about given up when she found the box behind the toy chest. In the confusion of moving the furniture, the valentines must have fallen off the dresser. Or maybe Ellen's little boys had been looking at them, thought Deanna. She gave Krissie an extra hug as she helped her into the day-care center van. "Happy Valentine's Day. Enjoy your party."

She dressed hurriedly. As she slipped on red earrings, she wished that it wasn't the store's busiest day in the year. She'd be waiting on customers all day without any time off for a lunch break.

As she walked to work, she couldn't tell whether it was still snowing lightly or whether the wind was tossing last night's snowfall into the air. At the back of her mind was the determination to place a call to Dr. Owens's office as soon as his office nurse was in. Thoughts of Reece made Valentine's Day a mockery.

She had just opened up the store when a United Federal delivery truck pulled up to the back door. No! Not more pottery. Her stomach tightened. Then she let out her breath in a sigh of relief when she saw that the driver was bringing in a small package about the size of a book. As he handed it to her, she was startled to see her name on the package instead of the store's. For a moment, she just stared at it. Then suddenly her hands were trembling.

"Why don't you open it, Foxy?" asked the husky young man standing at her elbow.

Foxy.

There was no time to react. His broad hand went over her mouth, and he jerked her back against him in a tight grip. She writhed helplessly in his arms as he whisked her out the back door and into the delivery truck.

It was impossible. Ridiculous. She'd hardly given the man more than a glance all the times he'd been in and out of the store.

He shoved her to the floor of the truck between stacks of boxes. She flayed her arms and legs in a fruitless effort to get free. A strangled cry broke from her lips as he tied a gag across her mouth that bit into the corners of her lips.

He rolled her over onto her stomach and securely bound her hands behind her, then tied her ankles together with the same piece of new, stiff rope. When he was finished, she was trussed securely. Like a fowl ready for slaughter.

"Happy Valentine's Day, darling."

He climbed out of the back of the truck and slammed the door shut, leaving her in murky darkness. The smell of dust, paper and grit filled her nostrils. The cloth across her mouth gagged her, and when she tried to move, the rope binding her wrists and ankles bit into her flesh like a searing poker.

He was gone for several minutes. Fear and panic battered her insides. Atrocities forced upon other women filled her frantic mind. He would assault her. Then kill her.

She heard the back door of the store close, then he climbed into the front seat. He turned around and called to her. "Everything's locked up nice and tight, Foxy. And I put a Closed sign in the window."

Deanna groaned. *Would anyone know what had happened?*

Her thoughts raced. Maybe Reece would come to the store to talk with her. He knew she was depending upon doing a brisk business on Valentine's Day. He would surely know something was wrong. Wouldn't he? No. After their last encounter, he wouldn't come near the store or try to get in touch with her.

Nellie was scheduled to come in early, at eleven o'clock instead of twelve, but she didn't have a key. Deanna was certain she'd try to reach her at home but when nobody answered, Deanna wasn't sure what the woman would do.

By then, it might be too late for anyone to do anything.

The truck's gears ground as the man shoved it in reverse and backed up in the alley. Then the vehicle moved forward. Noise and vibration accompanied the whirling of tires upon crushed snow. Traffic noises told her he was driving along city streets, but the dim interior gave her no hint of where they were or in what direction he was driving. When the stop-and-go movement changed and a steady roar of the engine indicated a higher speed, she knew they were no longer in Boulder.

Where was he taking her?

A sway of the truck indicated curves. New despair increased her panic. Last night, Reece had driven on the same kind of slippery serpentine road.

Boulder Canyon?

High mountain cliffs, heavy snow and myriad crevices pocketed rocky slopes and provided perfect cover for victims of violence. Many young women had lost their lives in the area between Boulder and the small mountain town of Nederland. Innocent victims just like herself. She didn't know why the man had picked her as his prey. Probably, he'd seen her walking home that night, recognized her from the store, and had decided that sooner or later he'd abduct her. There was no doubt in her mind that he planned to kill her.

She thought about Krissie and about the joy she would find in watching her daughter grow up. A pleasure that would be stolen from her if the cruel rope biting her flesh was an indication of what was to come. A rise of anger mingled with fear, sending adrenaline surging through her aching body. She wasn't going to let that happen.

REECE SAT in his private corner at the bookstore and watched snow collect on a nearby roof. After leaving Deanna's house the day before, he had driven to Winter Park and had worn himself out on the ski slopes. Physical exercise had always helped him to clear his thinking. Only this time it didn't work. When he returned to Boulder late that night, he was as exasperated and as angry with Deanna as he'd been that morning.

After a sleepless night, he wasn't any closer to understanding what had gone wrong. Apparently, her feelings for him were about as deep as a drop of water. The night they'd spent together had made her back off from any future commitment. Yet he wanted her as completely as any man wants the woman of his choice.

He let the legs of his tilted chair slam onto the floor. All right, if that's the way she wanted it. He sure as hell wasn't going to tag around after her like a lost puppy. He'd keep his distance. No telephone calls. No invitations for lunch. Nothing. He'd make himself scarce and see what happened. Maybe she'd realize that she couldn't have it both ways.

He was too old for adolescent relationships. And, he'd planned a grown-up surprise to celebrate Valentine's Day—but she'd made it plain enough that he wasn't her choice of a sweetheart.

DEANNA KNEW from the pitch of the truck that it was climbing a steep grade. An uneven, bouncing movement told her that they had left the highway. New fright crowded into her chest. She closed her eyes tightly as the slipping and sliding of the wheels told her they had lost traction. What if the truck plunged over the side of one of the cliffs?

She could picture the deep canyons and sheer rock walls that made driving so treacherous. One careless turn of the steering wheel could send a vehicle crashing thousands of feet below.

When the truck finally stopped, a wave of relief coated her fears for a split second. Then he jerked open the rear door, and terror returned. For a moment, she was blinded by bright light and luminous snow.

"Here we are, Foxy. Home sweet home."

He could have been delivering one of his packages for all the attention he paid her as he threw her over his shoulder and carried her into a small rustic cabin half-hidden by snow-laden pine trees. After kicking open the unlocked door, he took her into a small bedroom and dropped her on the bed.

Fiery stabs of pain shot through her body. Sobs crowded behind the cruel gag. Her bound arms and legs throbbed. When she felt his hands untying the rope around her wrists and ankles, tears of relief flowed into her eyes. But her comfort was short-lived. The next moment, he secured her hands above her head, tying her wrists to the bedstead. Then he put her feet together and tied her ankles to the iron foot railing. The only blessing was that he removed the gag.

"No need for that," he said as he tossed it aside. "You can yell your lungs out and nobody will hear you way up here. Now, I've got to go finish my route. But I'll be back."

He tossed the small unopened package on the bed. "It's a book. Enjoy yourself," he said with a mocking laugh.

"Please, don't do this. Let me go."

He gave a firm tug on the brim of his hat and pulled down his jacket over his long torso. His eyes were in shadow as he looked down at her. "Rest easy, sweetheart. We have some celebrating to do tonight. It's Valentine's Day, you know."

Chapter Seventeen

Reece spent the morning unpacking and taking an inventory of the books he'd bought in Colorado Springs. Several of them caught his eye, and he was able to lose himself for brief periods of time in the delight of scanning some rare and entertaining volumes. When lunchtime came, he bundled himself up in jacket and ski hat and headed to the College Kitchen.

As always, the place was crowded. With a sigh, he sat by himself trying to get rid of a nagging emptiness that food didn't seem to fill. He tried to read, but finally he set his book aside. Thoughts of Deanna intruded like a song that echoed in his mind. He remembered the day he had asked if he could share her table in this same café.

She had told him to get lost until he called her Dee Dee. Then her eyes had lit up with such joy that he thought the close feelings they'd always shared had been renewed. But he had been mistaken.

He ran an agitated hand through his hair. What in the hell had gone wrong? She had responded to his kisses and caresses with a fiery passion that had whirled them into a night of lovemaking. She had given herself to him with an open acceptance beyond his most intimate dreams.

But in the morning, all that had changed. She had flatly rejected the idea that they could mean something to each other. Her nervous keep-your-distance-from-me attitude had left him baffled—and angry. Maybe she was trying to make her ex-husband jealous. If the truth were known, maybe *she* was the one who wanted to get back together again and Brad wasn't interested. Who knew what in blazes was going on? He had opened his heart to her and been turned away, and he'd be damned if he'd let himself in for that kind of rejection again.

It was time that he thought about his own future. He'd been hoping that Deanna would be a part of any plans he made to finish his doctorate and try for a college teaching position at the nearby Colorado School of Mines. Time to wise up, fellow, he told himself. Cut loose from all his stupid what-might-have-been fantasies. Deanna had made it clear that she wanted no part of a permanent relationship. The way she had looked at him after their night of love was enough to hurt any man's pride. He was a slow learner when it came to affairs of the heart, but even he knew that it was time to get as far away from Boulder and Deanna Donovan as possible.

He finished his lunch without paying any attention to what he was eating. He was surprised to see Nellie Shaw come into the café when he was ready to leave. Reece knew the saleswoman came to work at noon, but because it was Valentine's Day, her schedule had probably been changed. He glanced at his watch. Twelve-thirty. She must be taking a lunch break. He wondered when Deanna had taken hers and then shoved the thought away. What in the hell did it matter? He was through trying to keep track of her. She wanted him out of her life. Good enough!

He paid his ticket and slammed out of the café. Valentine's Day. What a crock!

DEANNA LAY moaning on the narrow bed. She tried to move to relieve the pressure on her aching arms and legs, but there was very little slack in the rope tying her to the bed. Sharp pains shot through her wrists and ankles, and the chafing rope cut into her flesh with every move she made, creating raw bleeding sores that were like bands of searing fire.

She bit her lip and choked back hysterical sobs. She had to save her energy. Keep her mind clear. A good-size window gave her a view of the outside as she twisted her head at an uncomfortable angle. The position of the sun told her it must be about noon. She'd opened up the store at eight-thirty, so she'd been gone a little more than three hours. *Only three hours? An eternity.*

Her abductor had said he'd put a Closed sign in
the window. Surely someone would think that ominous on Valentine's Day. Wouldn't one of her customers notice and investigate. No, of course, they
wouldn't, an inner voice mocked. If the store was
closed, they would just take their business else-
where. Would Darrel notice the increase of business
and wonder why? Not likely. And she'd already dismissed Reece as someone who might try to find out
where she was. Her emotional blindness had driven
him away.

Nellie? Deanna closed her eyes and tried to think
what Nellie's reasoning would be.

First of all, the woman would be ticked off when
she found the store closed. She'd jump to the conclusion that Deanna was one of those irresponsible
young people she was always muttering about. The
store's busiest day in the year and Deanna couldn't
even get to work on time. Then she'd probably find
a phone and call the house. When no one answered,
what then? Would the woman wait around to see if
Deanna showed up? Or would she go back home?
Unless Nellie made someone aware of the unusual
situation, thought Deanna with new despair, the
store could remain locked up all day and no one
would even notice.

REECE HAD ALMOST made it back to the bookstore
when he heard someone calling his name.

"Mr. Ryndell—Mr. Ryndell."

He turned around. Nellie Shaw propelled her plump frame down the sidewalk toward him. A scarf whipped around her thick neck, and gray hair protruded from the edge of a wool hat. Clouds of vapor formed in front of her lips as she came puffing up to him. He knew from her expression something was wrong. Her agitation was obvious. For a fleeting moment, he wondered if she had been fired.

"I wonder if you could help me?" she gasped.

What on earth did the woman want from him, thought Reece as he nodded. If Deanna had fired her, there was little he could do. Maybe she was about to ask him for a job in the bookstore. He was already forming a polite rejection in his mind when she jerked his thoughts into a different direction.

"It's Mrs. Donovan. She hasn't opened the store today. I don't understand it at all. She planned this big Valentine's Day sale, and we've already lost half of a day. What on earth is the girl thinking of?"

Reece was instantly torn in two directions. What Deanna decided to do about opening and closing the store was none of his business. She'd made it clear to him that she was in charge of her life and intended to keep it that way. But if something unexpected had happened, she might need him. Familiar protective feelings sprang instantly to the fore. Even as he chided himself for being the fool, he asked, "Have you called Deanna at home?"

She nodded. "I did that first thing. Nobody answered. Then I waited around, checking the store every few minutes to see if she had shown up. Finally, I decided to get a cup of coffee and get warm. When I saw you..." Her voice faltered. "I thought maybe you'd know if she'd been called out of town unexpectedly."

"Not that I know of." His mind raced. Could Deanna have been so upset about what had happened between them that she couldn't face coming to work? "Maybe she's just not answering the phone."

"Because she's sick or something?"

The first flicker of uneasiness made his voice strident. "I don't know what she's up to, but I'll go by the house and find out."

"Oh, would you? I'd feel so much better. I mean, it seems kind of funny, doesn't it? She's been working so hard and nothing seems to go right. She's had a run of bad luck, that's for sure. Having the police in and out of the store makes me nervous." Her eyes rounded. "You don't think we ought to notify them, do you?"

"No, I'm sure there's a simple explanation. Why don't you go home, and I'll have Deanna call you."

"Thank you." The expression on her face wavered between relief and disgust. "You'd think she'd take care of the store in memory of her parents, if nothing else."

REECE HAD no idea what he was going to say to Deanna when she answered the door. He certainly didn't want her to think that he was there to plead

with her. She knew he loved her. What more could he
say? What more could he do? As he mounted the
front steps, he called himself a fool for being there.
If she had decided to close the store for a day, it was
none of his business.

His knock was brisk.

A startled look crossed Nicki's face when she
opened the door and saw who it was. She must have
just arrived home for she was in the process of taking off her jacket. "You?" She swallowed. "What
do you want?"

"Deanna. Is she home?"

"No. Go away." She started to shut the door.

Reece was too quick for her. He was inside before
she could stop him. She gave a frightened gasp.
"Leave or I'll call the police."

"I want to talk to Deanna." He glanced up the
staircase, debating whether to storm upstairs and
make a scene if he found her. "Where is she?"

Nicki backed away from him. "At the store."

"No, she isn't."

"If she's not at the store, I don't know where she
is."

Reece had the feeling that the girl was telling the
truth so he forced himself to speak pleasantly.
"What about this morning, Nicki? Did she say anything about her plans?"

"No." Her frightened eyes belied her denial.

"You're lying." He forgot all about being pleasant. "What plans did she have for the day?"

Nicki cowered. "I don't know. I want you to leave."

"I'm not going anywhere until you quit lying. I'm running out of patience, Nicki." He grabbed her by the shoulders. "Tell me now."

"She was going to call Dr. Owens."

Reece's mind raced. What had happened to send her to the doctor? He cursed himself for not checking on her yesterday. His damned pride had kept him away. He dropped his hands from Nicki's shoulder. "What's the matter with her? Why was she going to see Dr. Owens?"

Nicki's chin thrust forward. "I told her she should go to the police instead of the doctor."

"Police? Dr. Owens? What in blazes is going on?"

Her eyes flashed. "You know."

Reece grabbed her arm. "If I knew, I wouldn't be asking you, would I?"

Nicki moistened her dry lips. "She wanted to get you some help."

"Me?"

Nicki's eyes opened wider with fear. "She wanted Dr. Owens to know everything about you before she called the police."

His voice was strangely calm considering the hurricane beginning to build inside his head. "Wanted the doctor to know *what* about me?"

"About the crazy things you've been doing."

Reece stared at her for a long, quiet moment. "She thinks I'm the one who's been doing all that crazy stuff? I don't believe it. She wouldn't have let me stay the other night, if that had been the case."

"She didn't know—until you got up in the night and moved all Krissie's furniture around."

"I did what?"

His utter surprise seemed to disconcert her. "You did, didn't you? Move all the things? Put them back the way the room was when Deanna was growing up?"

"Hell, no. Why would she think such a thing?"

"Nobody else could have moved all the furniture in the middle of the night," Nicki insisted. "If it wasn't you, who could it have been?"

Chapter Eighteen

Sergeant McDowell listened without comment as Reece told him on the phone about the weird happenings inside Deanna's house on Saturday night.

"Why didn't she report it?"

"Because she thought I was responsible. But more importantly, her store is closed. Either she didn't open it this morning or she decided to close it before eleven o'clock when her help got there."

"We'll check it out. Stay at her house until we get there."

"Maybe she's at the doctor's office," Nicki suggested. "I mean, she could have decided to go there first—and got detained." She flashed an accusing look at Reece, easily read. *This is all your fault.*

A call to Dr. Owens's office brought a negative response. Mrs. Donovan had not contacted the office that morning.

Nicki slumped on the sofa and nervously twisted her hair while Reece paced the room. He couldn't believe it. Deanna was convinced he was mentally ill. No wonder she had acted frightened and distant. Dammit, why hadn't she said something, accused him of trying to drive her nuts, and voiced her concern? Instead, she planned to go behind his back to Dr. Owens. And no wonder. What hell she must have gone through. Convinced he'd moved the furniture around in the night, she had decided that he was responsible for everything else that had happened to her.

Reece's blood suddenly ran cold. Someone else had been in the house that night. When he got up to go to the bathroom, he had heard night noises but thought that it was the wind and snow hitting the outside of the house. Had the intruder been in the house at that moment? If only he had gone to investigate. Instead, he had slipped back into bed and gathered Deanna in his arms. Later, she must have thought that's when he'd been in Krissie's room.

When Sergeant McDowell arrived with Officer Hanks, Reece met them at the door. "What did you find at the store?"

"All locked up just as you said," McDowell answered. "We got a key from the locksmith who put in the new locks, and looked around."

Hanks held out Deanna's winter coat and purse. "This is what we found."

"Where would she go without her coat and purse?" Nicki asked in a tight voice. Her anxious gaze swept the faces of the three men. "Are you sure she wasn't in the bathroom—or somewhere?"

McDowell didn't reply. Reece's heart took a sickening dive. "So she was there this morning."

The officer took out his pad and pencil. "All right. Tell me when Mrs. Donovan left the house this morning."

Nicki chewed her lip. "I'm not sure. I mean, I left while she was still getting Krissie ready. Mornings are bedlam around here. I guess she left at the same time. Or maybe a little bit earlier. I know she was dreading a hectic Valentine's Day. That's the store's busiest day and—"

"Did she mention anything else?"

Nicki glared at Reece. "She was going to call Dr. Owens first thing."

"About what?"

"About me," Reece snapped. "I told you on the phone. She thought I was responsible for moving stuff around in the middle of the night on Saturday."

"Dee didn't want to turn him over to the police until she'd spoken with his doctor," Nicki added.

"And you didn't do it?" McDowell asked in a neutral tone.

Worry, anger and impatience made Reece want to shout at the officer to quit asking stupid questions and wasting time. With great effort, he answered, "No. Someone must have come into the house either while we were out to dinner or while we were asleep and moved the bedroom furniture. Deanna discovered it in the morning and jumped to the conclusion that I'd done it."

McDowell told Officer Hanks to look around the house, inside and out. Then he asked. "The doors were all locked and bolted?"

Reece nodded. "I checked them myself before going upstairs."

"Then how did anyone get in?"

"I don't know, but it happened."

"Even if someone had a key, the new bolt locks would have to be opened from the inside. Were you in the house Saturday night, miss?"

Nicki shook her blond head. "No, I was with some friends skiing. And Krissie was with her father. So Deanna was alone—with him."

Reece's patience snapped. "Is all of this necessary, Sergeant McDowell? Shouldn't you be spending your time looking for Deanna, instead of wasting time talking about Saturday night? She's missing, dammit."

"I've put an all-points out on Mrs. Donovan. I have people checking with all the nearby stores, asking if anybody saw her or noticed anyone else who was hanging around this morning. She's not a missing person for twenty-four hours, you know. If it wasn't for the recent police reports, I'd wait until tomorrow to put out a search for her. If she's wandering around town, we'll find her soon enough. And if she isn't—" his bushy eyebrows matted "—then we need to find out everything we can about what's been going on."

Officer Hanks came back and reported that the blowing snow had obliterated any tracks that might have been outside.

"No sign of any broken windows." He scratched his head. "One thing, though. In the basement. Looks like some snow might have drifted in because there's a puddle in the old coal bin. Couldn't see how it got there since the coal chute is boarded up."

"Coal chute?" Reece echoed.

"Does that mean something to you?" McDowell demanded.

Reece stared at the officer. His mind pulled at a memory long forgotten. Images, clear and stark, sprang up full-blown. "When the house was converted to gas heating, the coal chute at the back of the house was boarded up. When we were kids, it was easy enough to push up the board lid, slide down the chute and sneak up the basement stairs. Once Deanna even had a Halloween party and everyone had to come in that way."

"Gee, how creepy," Nicki mumbled.

Reece's stomach churned. "If that chute is still usable, entrance into the house at any time is a simple matter."

DEANNA THOUGHT a lot about Reece as she fought waves of pain during the long afternoon. She remembered tiny things about him: the way his eyes softened when he looked at her; the soft curve of a smile when he was amused at something she'd said; the quiet chuckle that would suddenly change to merry laughter.

How could she have mistrusted him? He had always been there for her. Even when she had become infatuated with Brad and had shut Reece out of her life, he had gone on loving her. And now, when she desperately loved and needed him, her stupid suspicions had driven him away. There was no reason for him even to be aware of the horrible thing that had happened to her. His pride would keep him from trying to see her again.

Forgive me, Reece, she thought as tears ran down her cheeks. She'd been under too much pressure to think clearly. Even now, she couldn't understand what had happened. Why had she become the focus of a demented man who had viciously tormented her before abducting her? She'd never really looked at the deliveryman closely, nor had any personal interest in him. He was just someone who came in and out of the store bringing packages. He must have done the same when her parents were alive. *Her parents!* Had her parents dismissed him as indifferently as she had done, letting him into the store after hours? Even though the police had said robbery was probably the motive, her father's wallet was left in his pocket.

Until that moment, she had believed that all the things that had happened to her were random acts.

With horrifying insight, she now realized that they had been deliberately and viciously planned.

The hours passed with agonizing slowness. Late afternoon, the sound of a car laboring up the road jerked her eyes to the window. Through the snowy branches of needled trees, she glimpsed a car turning around at the end of a clearing and then coming back to stop in front of the cabin.

The man driving an old blue Chevy had returned.

Chapter Nineteen

The kidnapper was still in uniform and wearing his hat when he came in. Without saying anything, he walked over to the narrow bed and untied the knotted rope holding her arms above her head. As she lowered them, stretched muscles contracted in excruciating spasms, and her arms felt as if they were being pulled from their sockets. She cried out in pain, and unbidden tears flowed down her cheeks.

"Cut the tears!" he growled. His broad hand lashed out. "I don't like sniffling females. I finished my route early so I could get back to you."

Then he untied her ankles and pulled her to her feet.

She bit her lower lip, stifling her cries. Her legs gave way and he held her upright in his thick arms as he pulled her across the room.

Where was he taking her? She struggled to stiffen her body as he opened a narrow door and shoved her into a small bathroom. She fell against a sink and held on to it for support.

"Get beautiful, sweetheart. We're going to have a party."

He slammed the door shut and turned a key. She hung her head over a small, chipped sink where a corroded faucet dripped water into the stained basin, sounding like the ticking of a clock.

Don't pass out.

Her body reeled with pain. Light-headed from fright and a day spent on her back, she clung to the old sink to keep from sliding to the floor. Slowly, her balance returned. She managed to turn on the water, splash her face and wash the blood from her bleeding wrists. The ice-cold water revived her somewhat. Pain began to ease from her limbs. Cautiously, she put more weight on her legs as she straightened up.

She looked at her reflection in a small mirror above the sink, aghast at the ravages of her abduction. Her eyes were shadowed, her cheeks puffy and ugly deep lines marred the edges of her mouth. Tangled hair hung around her face, and as she brushed back the matted strands, she saw a bruise forming on her cheek where he had hit her.

Get beautiful, he had ordered.

Silent hysterical laughter rumbled in her chest. Then raw panic silenced the mirth as she looked around desperately for a weapon. She jerked open the door of a wooden medicine chest, praying for a razor, a pair of scissors, anything that might offer the means to escape with her life.

Nothing but a half-used tube of toothpaste, a small battery-operated shaver and a pill bottle with two tablets left in it. There was no cupboard under the sink, just bare pipes disappearing into the dirty white wall.

The shower stall was empty of everything except a bar of soap and a musty-smelling washrag. Two gray towels hung on the rack, and a nearly finished roll of toilet paper was sitting on a stool. The bathroom must have been converted from a shed connected to the house because there were no windows and a ventilator about the size of a notebook was the only opening in the room.

A rising sense of claustrophobia churned her stomach, but she frantically sought a way to lock herself in the small room. She was willing to do anything to keep him from getting at her again. But there was no way to escape and no way to keep him out.

She pressed back against the wall, hysterical sobs rising in her chest.

I don't like sniffling females.

She could hear him moving around in the bedroom. What was he doing? What did he have planned?

We're going to have a party.

Any hope that she could appeal to him on a rational level was gone. A party! Only a demented mind would arrange such a horror. He had planned it, as he must have planned everything else that had happened to her, as he orchestrated the terror against her. And now the waiting game was over.

"Are you about ready for some fun, Foxy?"

She covered her mouth to keep from screaming.

REECE WENT AROUND the outside of Deanna's house with the officers. Snow had blown over the cover of the coal chute and had covered up any footprints that might have been there on Saturday or Sunday. Officer Hanks tried to lift the heavy cover and couldn't. Both policemen looked ready to discount the idea that someone had lifted it in order to get into the house.

"You can't move it that way...." Reece said quickly. "You slide it up, like this." He took hold of the lid and pushed on it. The board cover moved upward until it hit the exterior of the house, leaving a space that was about half the size of the original opening. The passage wasn't even dusty!

Without waiting for an order from McDowell, Reece raised himself by resting his hands on both sides of the chute, shoved his feet out in front of him and disappeared down the metal chute. A child's game with deadly impact.

He waited at the bottom for the other two men. Officer Hanks came first and then McDowell.

"Someone could have gotten in that way, all right," said Hanks as the three of them stood at the bottom of the entrance.

"Who knew about this way into the house?" McDowell asked Reece.

"Many people through the years, I'd guess. I told you, a lot of the neighborhood kids certainly did. Anyway, it's common knowledge that most of these old houses had coal furnaces at one time. Anyone could figure out that a house in this neighborhood might be accessible through an old chute."

"But how many burglars would know about the exact way to get it open?" McDowell centered his skeptical gaze on Reece. "You had to show Hanks how to do it."

Something in his tone made Reece snap angrily, "You think I'm making all this up, don't you? Instead of looking for the weirdo who's been coming in and out of the house at will, you're wasting valuable time accusing me."

"All things considered," McDowell answered evenly, "I think we should go down to the station so we can continue our little chat, Mr. Ryndell."

"But what about Deanna? You should be spending your time looking for her, not harassing me!"

"Maybe you can help us find her. Did you by any chance happen to drop by the store this morning? Maybe you talked her into going somewhere."

"I told you. I haven't seen her since Sunday morning. I didn't even know the store was closed until Nellie Shaw told me." Worry over Deanna threatened Reece's usual self-control. He clenched his fists and bit back some colorful words. He knew the policeman was doing his job—baiting him and being suspicious of everything he said—but every minute lost might be crucial to Deanna's safety.

As Reece was leaving with the two officers, the day-care van delivered Krissie. Nicki took charge of her the way she always did, but Reece could tell that the girl was distraught. She didn't seem the type to handle an emergency very well. "I think you ought to assign a female officer to the house until Deanna is located," he told McDowell.

The policeman just grunted. "The department doesn't provide baby-sitters."

While Reece was at the station, Brad was escorted in by a couple of officers. He didn't have any more information to offer than Reece. The last time he'd seen Deanna was on Sunday when he had brought Krissie home. He didn't seem especially worried. "So she locked up the store. My guess is that she decided to give herself a day off."

No, that's what you would do, Reece thought when they met in the hallway and Brad repeated what he'd said to the police. Reece knew that Deanna wouldn't jeopardize the success of the store by closing on Valentine's Day. He told Brad as much.

He shrugged. "Deanna doesn't like to have a fuss made over her. She'll blow a fuse when she finds out you've called in the police." Brad scowled. "Maybe you should have minded your own business, Reece."

"Deanna *is* my business," he said, leveling his icy gray eyes at Brad. Then he walked away before he could vent his anger on Brad's handsome smug face.

It was late afternoon when McDowell released Reece. The day was almost gone and there was still no sign of Deanna when he returned to her house and found Nicki jumpy and unable to settle anywhere. His hopes that Deanna had called were dashed with a shake of Nicki's head.

"Have the police found out anything?" she asked anxiously.

"They're still looking. Deanna must have left the store with someone."

"Not Tony," she said quickly as though she'd already been over the possibility that her ex-boyfriend might have been involved. "His father's ill. He had to go home for a few days. His family lives in New Mexico."

Krissie grabbed Reece's legs and started to cry. Reece picked her up and took her for a pony ride on his shoulders. She was laughing when he set her down, but her face quickly puckered up. "Where's Mommy?" she whined. "I want my mommy."

With a child's perception, she had picked up on Nicki's anxiety. The little girl knew something was wrong and refused to be distracted. Her breathing was punctuated by a dry cough.

"I don't know what I'll do if she gets sick on me. Maybe I ought to call her father."

"Brad knows that Deanna is missing. He was at the police station. If he wanted to take care of his daughter, he would be here," Reece snapped. "Why don't you call Mrs. Caruthers to keep you company? Deanna said that she was going to have her baby-sit for her sometime."

"I don't know her."

"Well, I do. She's a neighbor and her daughter was Deanna's best friend."

"I know. Deanna said Ellen was here with her two bratty little boys. I guess they nearly tore up the house the way Ellen's kid brothers used to do."

Reece stared at her. "What did you say?"

Nicki raised her voice. "I said that Ellen Caruthers's two kids nearly tore up the place the way Ellen's brothers used to do."

Reece swung on his heels and started for the door.

"Where are you going?" Nicki picked up Krissie and followed him into the hall.

He just gave a wave of his hand and bounded out the door. Richard Caruthers! Why hadn't he thought of him the minute they'd discovered someone had been using the coal chute? A year older than Deanna and Ellen, his sister, Richard had pestered the two girls in every way possible. It all came back to Reece with appalling clarity.

Richard! Once, he had let himself into the house and sneaked up to Deanna's bedroom where the girls were doing their nails and trying on dresses. They'd been furious and reported him to Deanna's parents.

A couple of times, Reece had even gone to talk to Mrs. Caruthers about the way Richard had tormented Deanna on the way to high school when she was a freshman.

"Richard's a handful, all right," his mother had admitted. "But he only teases people he likes—and he likes Deanna. 'Course, she doesn't pay him any mind, unless he's pestering her." She had given a short laugh. "I guess he'll do about anything to make her notice him."

Reece's mind raced like a computer searching a disk for information. Everything had pointed to someone who had been in the old neighborhood gang. Who else would know how the furniture had been arranged in Deanna's room? And who else besides someone from the past would make use of the coal chute entrance? Only someone like Richard Caruthers.

When Deanna had returned to Boulder, Richard must have decided to take up from where he'd left off, when she spurned his attentions as a teenager. Who knew how far that twisted mind of his would go if he had Deanna in his power?

Reece's lungs burned with the cold air as he plunged through drifted snow. A nervous heat caused sweat to break out on his forehead. The Carutherses' house sat back from the street with tall spruce and pine trees crowding the snow-filled yard. Tire tracks showed that a car had recently been driven out of the old garage.

Reece bounded up the weathered steps. His loud knocking brought Mr. Caruthers to the door. "Come in, Reece. Come in. I've been suffering from a cold and my help's running the station. Ellen's here with her two kids. Her and the missus went shopping. You know how it is with womenfolk. They—"

Reece cut him off. "I'm here to ask about Richard. Where is he?"

"Come on into the kitchen. I was about to open up a beer." He turned his back on Reece and shuffled into the next room. Reece followed. "Grab a chair."

"I don't have time. It's very important that I locate Richard right away."

Mr. Caruthers brought out two cans of beer. "Sit down and rest yourself."

"Please, answer me. Where can I find your son?"

Mr. Caruthers popped open a beer can before he answered. "I thought everybody knew." He took a swig of beer and then met Reece's eyes. "Richard got in a bit of trouble. Selling drugs, he was. He's been in jail for the last year."

Chapter Twenty

The bathroom door jerked open. He had changed out of his deliveryman's uniform and wore faded denim pants and a red-checkered flannel shirt. For an instant, his face seemed vaguely familiar. Under normal circumstances, she might have put a name to the face immediately. Now, raw fear blotted out everything but the way he pinned her arms at her sides and pulled her from the bathroom.

"You look a mess. I'll brush your hair and put a ribbon in it. A red one for Valentine's Day. You always looked pretty with a bow in your hair."

He shoved her down into a sitting position on the floor. Then he sat on the bed and held her securely between his legs while he brushed her hair. He sang softly as he stroked the tangled strands. "My funny valentine...my sweet funny valentine...don't change a thing for me...."

A nightmare. This couldn't be happening. His grotesque tenderness was more frightening than the slap on her face. She recoiled from his touch and choked back cries of pain as her matted hair caught in the brush. Sometimes he pulled her head back with a cruel jerk. He looped her hair over one hand as he brushed it with the other one, counting up to fifty.

He seemed to be in no hurry. Stroke after stroke, he smoothed her hair. Sometimes he stopped and slipped a curl over his finger, laughing softly as he played with it. She could have been a doll, an inanimate object.

She was afraid to say anything. Afraid to move. She didn't dare challenge him. His hands were only inches from her neck. At any moment, he could put steel fingers around her throat and choke the life from her body.

Finally, he fumbled in his pocket and brought out a huge, red velvet bow. He grabbed a hank of hair on the top of her head and clumsily fastened the bow's clip. He fiddled with it to get the ribbon standing up the way he wanted. Then he grunted with satisfaction. "Now you look pretty. Just the way you did that Easter when you wore that red polka-dot dress. Remember?"

Polka-dot dress? She vaguely remembered a dress like that. How old had she been? Fourteen?

"Time to party." He pulled her to her feet and roughly pushed her into the knotty-pine front room.

The sight that met her eyes made her gasp with disbelief. Red and white paper streamers hung in swags the length of the room. Valentine hearts trimmed with white lace decorated the walls, paper cupids hung by strings from the ceiling and vases of artificial red roses adorned the fireplace mantel. A table placed in the middle of the floor was laden with chocolates, a party cake and a bottle of cheap wine. Two red candles matched the paper tablecloth and party napkins.

"How do you like it?" he asked, keeping his iron grip on her.

"It's . . . very pretty," she croaked.

"I did it for you. Tonight we celebrate. You're going to be my very own sweetheart forever and ever."

Forever and ever. He was mad. If she'd ever doubted his intentions to kill her, his chilling words dispelled her thoughts.

REECE LEFT the Carutherses' house like someone who had been racing madly ahead only to discover the earth had fallen away in front of him. The fact that Richard's imprisonment eliminated him as a suspect had brought Reece to a screeching halt.

He tried to think of other fellows who had been about Deanna's age at the time and could have known about the cellar entrance. He went back to the police station and asked to see the photos that they had dusted for fingerprints. As Reece went over them, he made a list of everyone he could identify in the party photographs. Many of the names escaped him. Kids had moved in and out of the neighborhood all the time. Maybe one of them had moved back. He brushed a moist hand over his forehead. *But which one?*

He picked up a photograph taken downtown at Christmas. A group of carolers, which included Deanna and Ellen, were singing in front of an outdoor Christmas tree. One of the singers in the back row caught his eye. He looked at the man closely and then added Darrel Evans to the list.

"Come up with anything?" McDowell asked, looking over Reece's shoulder.

Reece shook his head. "I've made a list of everyone I can identify. Even the adults. Have your men checked out Darrel Evans? Maybe he sent Deanna on a wild-goose chase. It would be to his advantage to keep her store closed on Valentine's Day."

McDowell gave Reece an irritated look. "We talked to him first thing. He came to work at five a.m. with two of his employees and didn't leave the store all morning. If he took time out to kidnap his competition, I don't know how he did it. Assuming Mrs. Donovan was kidnapped. I wouldn't be surprised if she didn't come back from a day's shopping in Denver and be 'oh so sorry' she didn't tell anyone."

"Deanna's not like that. Something's happened to her. I know it!" A new surge of anxiety made his voice unsteady.

At that moment, Officer Hanks came in. "We just got a report from one of the officers working the mall. Someone who works in the bank was passing Dee's Candy and Gift Shop about nine o'clock this morning and saw a delivery truck parked out in back. She said an Open sign was in the window when she passed.''

"Get on it. Find out which company made a delivery there today.''

"Yes, sir.''

Reece was out of his chair and heading for the door.

"Where are you going?'' McDowell called after him.

He just waved his hand and didn't answer. Nagging impressions that he'd ignored before came crashing to the front of his mind. If he was right, the answer had been in front of them all the time.

Chapter Twenty-One

He forced Deanna to sit in a wooden chair at the table. He loomed over her, sitting close enough to land a harsh blow to her head if she made any resistance to his wishes.

"Give me some cake," he ordered, handing her two gaily decorated paper plates that matched the party tablecloth. The cake had already been cut into squares, and a small plastic server lay beside it. "Two pieces, with lots of frosting. Don't be stingy."

Don't be stingy. She froze. The order triggered a memory. *Don't be stingy. Don't be stingy.* The words and the voice had a familiar ring. She looked up at him. A flicker of recognition deepened. The shape of his head and facial bone structure were familiar, but not the hard cheeks and firm chin. Then she knew what was wrong. There was no fat hanging from his jowls, all excess weight was gone from his torso, arms and legs. Ellen Caruthers's younger brother was no longer fat.

"Benny!"

His face broke into a wide grin. "Now, you remember me."

It couldn't be. Not obese little Benny who had been so obnoxious when she was growing up. He'd hung around her and Ellen, pestering them at every opportunity.

As quickly as the smile came to Benny's face, it disappeared. His eyes took on a flinty dullness and his mouth grew hard. "All those years you ignored me because I was fat."

The memory of his obesity was suddenly very clear. His body had rolled from side to side when he walked, and pounds of fat jiggled on his arms and legs. Everyone tried to get him to cut down on his eating but he was a glutton.

"You thought I was ugly, didn't you?"

Deanna knew her life depended upon lying to him. "No, I didn't. I—"

"Don't lie! You hated it when I came around." He sank his fingers into her soft shoulders and shook her. She winced from the pain as her head bounced back and forth. When he stopped shaking her, he kept his fingers tightened cruelly on her shoulders. "You could have paid some attention to me. You and Ellen used to run off and hide from me. 'Go tell Mom she wants you,' Ellen used to say to me, and you'd laugh."

She tried to appease him. "Benny, you were younger than I—"

"Only three years. You didn't even notice when I grew up. I was a freshman in high school when you were a senior, and you never even smiled at me in the halls. And all the time you were my secret sweetheart."

"I'm sorry, Benny. Really I am. You have to understand that I didn't mean to hurt you." She moistened her dry lips. Now that she knew who he was, she felt stronger, more in control. She understood the source of his anger. Maybe it wasn't too late to play up to his wounded vanity. She couldn't believe that he would actually harm her. His next words swept away that misapprehension.

"I had to kill your folks so you'd come back."

She clutched the edge of the table in a wave of dizziness. Shock made her close her eyes. She couldn't believe it. Not someone who had known her parents so well. Her dad had always taken the time to talk to the neighborhood kids. She knew he would have let Benny into the store after hours without giving it a moment's thought. They would have accepted him as a friend—up to the moment he shot them.

"They wanted you to stay here, and so did I, but you wouldn't," Benny lashed out at her. "After Christmas, you left again. It's your fault I had to kill them."

A fury she'd never known before exploded within her. Her head jerked up. "No!" she shouted at him. "You murdered two wonderful, kind people. How could you do it? They were good to you, Benny. They put up with a lot from you for a good many years. Even when they caught you sneaking around the house, eating everything in sight, they never did anything but scold you. Why would you do such a horrible thing to them?''

"I knew you'd inherit the store, move back into the house and everything would be as it was before. Only this time you'd notice me. Even when you didn't pay any attention to me when I made deliveries, I knew that we were going to be together on Valentine's Day. I had it all planned. Foxy was my secret name for you. I wanted you to know I was around, so I did all that crazy stuff.'' He laughed. ''How'd you like all those dead roses on your car? And the box of candy? And the valentine stuck to your door?''

"You put the teddy bear in the chair. Moved all the furniture in Krissie's room.'' She stared at him in bewilderment. ''How did you get in and out of the house when I had the locks changed?''

He told her then about the coal chute. ''My own private entrance and exit, anytime I wanted.''

The cunning of his calculated harassment sent her blood running cold. ''You even ordered the pottery and then destroyed it.''

''Right. I wanted to keep making deliveries to the store, so I swiped some order blanks and some papers with your dad's signature. I wrote down the number of your father's credit card and then left his wallet in his pocket. Smart, huh?'' His face crinkled with mirth. "You should have seen your face when I kept bringing all that stuff in. I almost laughed out loud. You never looked me straight in the face." His laughter died. Anger brought color rushing into his cheeks. "But I knew that you'd pay plenty of attention to me when the time came."

"Benny, I'm sorry—"

"I don't want to talk anymore. I want to celebrate. First we'll eat . . . and then we'll dance . . . and then we'll make love. Remember all the parties in our basement? You never danced with me once in all those years. But tonight you're all mine. I waited a long time to make you all mine." He put his leering face close to hers. "I've waited a long time to do lots of things to you, sweetheart." Then he drew back. "But first we eat." He shoved a box of candy from her own store under her nose. "Have a chocolate."

With trembling fingers, she took one.

"Now some cake, cookies and wine."

When both plates were loaded with cake, chocolates and heart-shaped cookies, he handed her a glass of red wine and insisted on clicking the glasses together. "To us, Benny and Foxy, sweethearts forever!"

Deanna's stomach threatened to send bitter bile up into her mouth as she dutifully took a sip of the wine and nibbled on a cookie. There were no forks or knives, nothing at all that resembled a feeble weapon. She watched him out of the corner of her eye as he used his fingers to devour the sickeningly sweet refreshments.

"You're not eating," he accused her.

"I'm not—" she began.

He grabbed a chocolate and shoved it into her mouth. She began to gag. Then he picked up the wineglass and spilled the liquid over her lips and chin as he poured it into her mouth. She fought back a retching reflex, turned her head away from him and covered her mouth.

"All right, if you don't want to eat, we'll dance," he said in a petulant tone. He jerked her to her feet and turned on a small radio. An "oldies" station poured music into the small room. A baritone was crooning a love song.

He held her tightly against him as he clumsily moved his feet. A fierce light shone in his eyes as he looked down at her. Shuffling back and forth without rhythm, his movements were a pretense of dancing.

The last time Deanna had been dancing, it had been with Reece. They had moved together with the music, their bodies responding to each other's touch, their eyes locked in promises of love. Hot tears streamed down her face. She tried to hide them as Benny jerked her around the room.

The long confinement tied to the bed had sapped her strength. She'd had nothing to eat all day. She stumbled, and muffled a cry when his heavy gunboat feet came down harshly on hers. His firm hand splayed across her back like a clamp, pressing them together.

He stopped dancing and tightened his grip upon her. She felt the lust surging through him.

"No, Benny. Please—no."

Chapter Twenty-Two

Something that Mr. Caruthers had said during Reece's earlier visit brought him back to the neighbor's house. An old Buick stood in the driveway and the house was brightly lighted. Mrs. Caruthers and Ellen were home from their shopping trip. The older woman opened the door.

"Reece, how nice," she cooed. "It's been ages since you came around. And now twice in one day. Henry said you were here earlier. You came to say hello to Ellen." She turned around and called, "Ellen! Ellen! Come see who's here."

"No, I came to—"

"To visit with my big girl," she finished for him as she urged him into the living room, announcing, "Here's an old friend come to see you, Ellen. Doesn't my girl look great, Reece? And these are her two little boys. They're going to be a handful, just like my two."

"Hello, Reece." Ellen held out her hand. "Glad to see you. It's been a long time." She made no pretense about the measuring look she gave him. "Are you all right? I asked Deanna about you, but she was kind of vague. But I did get the impression she was worried about you. Are you two on the outs?"

"Now, Ellen, you know I don't hold with gossiping," her mother said without blinking an eyelid. "Whatever is going on with Reece and Deanna is none of our business. Come on and sit down a spell, Reece. You and Ellen can talk about old times and I'll put some water in the soup. You'll stay for a bite to eat, won't you?"

Before Reece could answer, Mr. Caruthers came in from the kitchen, unable to mask his surprise. The creases in his weathered face deepened.

"Reece? I thought that was your voice. You got some more questions about Richard?"

"Why was he asking about Richard?" Mrs. Caruthers's expression showed a sudden flash of anxiety. Obviously, bad news about her eldest son was not a new thing.

Reece ignored her and leveled his questions at her husband. "When I was here before, Henry, you told me that Benny had a steady job driving a truck. I thought you meant a big rig, a semi."

"No." He shook his gray head. "Benny couldn't handle one of them big jobs."

"He could, too," snapped his wife. "You always did sell Benny short. No wonder he moved out on us.

You two fighting all the time. Benny's always been a good boy. Look how he straightened himself out. Losing all that weight. Why, he—"

Reece cut her off with a slice of his hand. "What kind of a truck does Benny drive?"

"One of them United Federal panel trucks," Mr. Caruthers answered.

The floor under Reece's feet dipped. His stomach took a sickening plunge. A truck like that had been seen parked behind the store that morning, when the Open sign had been in the window. The truck had been seen in the alley. When Nellie arrived for work at eleven, the Closed sign was in the window.

"Why? Is there something wrong?" Mr. Caruthers asked as thick gray eyebrows matted over the bridge of his nose.

Reece had to take a deep breath to steady his voice. "We need to ask Benny some questions. What's his address?"

"You're sure he's all right," Mrs. Caruthers prodded.

"Yes. Where does he live?"

"Up the canyon. Between Boulder and Nederland. He's got a nice little place."

"He rented one of those cabins built back in the sixties. You know, when the canyon was overrun with flower children," Ellen offered.

An isolated mountain cabin! No wonder the police hadn't found Deanna. It was miles from Boulder to Nederland, with a hundred side roads. She could be anywhere. Alive or dead.

"Give me directions," Reece snapped. "Where's his place located?"

"We ain't never been there," Mr. Caruthers answered with an edge of regret in his voice. "When Benny moved out, he didn't put out the welcome mat to any of us. He's called his mother a few times and that's all. Doesn't even buy his gas from me."

"Are you sure something hasn't happened to Benny?" Benny's mother's voice was filled with parental anxiety. "He's not hurt, is he?"

"We have to find him, Mrs. Caruthers. Right away."

"What's he done?" Mr. Caruthers demanded, his jaw suddenly working as if he were bracing himself for the worst.

"I'm damn sure he's the one who's been stalking Deanna. And this morning, he abducted her."

IT WAS six o'clock. All the municipal buildings were closed. McDowell swore as he tried to raise somebody in the business office of the Public Service Company of Colorado.

He had listened to Reece's deductive reasoning and had nodded. "If the same person who took her is the same one who has been tormenting her, Benny Caruthers looks like our man."

"It has to be him. Everything fits. He knew how to get in and out of the house. He's been delivering stuff to the store, and his truck was seen in the alley about the time Deanna must have disappeared." Reece's voice rose. "We've got to bring him in."

"You don't have to convince me," McDowell said evenly. "What we have to do first is find out where in the hell the guy lives. We ought to be able to get his address from the utilities company."

Reece forced himself to sit down and quit pacing like a caged animal. The police knew how to handle these things. He'd given them the lead they needed. It wouldn't be long before they'd have Benny's address and would be on their way. He clenched his hands. He'd never thought of himself as being violent before, but he knew that if Benny Caruthers walked in the door that minute, he'd leap at him like a wild animal.

McDowell spent a frustrating fifteen minutes trying to locate someone who could check the gas and electricity records. The local office was closed and all the personnel had left the building.

The officer slammed down the phone. "I've left messages all over the place. No one has arrived home yet. As soon as someone calls back, I'll send them back to the office and we'll get a look at those computers. I've already tried the telephone company. No Benny Caruthers listed."

Reece glanced at his wristwatch. Deanna had been gone ten hours. "Hell, we've wasted too much time. I don't know why I didn't suspect Benny when I was at the Carutherses' the first time. His dad told me he was driving a truck and wasn't living in town anymore. I figured he was long gone from Boulder, driving a rig across the country." Reece slapped a fist into the palm of his other hand. "Stupid! Stupid! I should have paid attention to that fat little kid in all the pictures. Always hanging around. Tormenting the life out of his sister and Deanna. We all tried to ignore that repulsive kid as much as possible."

McDowell frowned. "Sounds like he's been building up a lot of pressure to get noticed."

"I'm afraid you're right. If only we'd handled him differently—"

"It's too late to be spending time on what can't be changed," McDowell snapped. "Hanks is working on a list of Benny's co-workers. They might give us a lead."

"Here they are, Sarge, the names and addresses of all the United Federal deliverymen in the area. Benny's route included Boulder and the small towns of Lafayette and Louisville. His supervisor says Benny uses a P.O. box for his private mail. And the only address on any of his forms is that of his parents."

"Maybe one of his co-workers knows where he lives. Call the drivers who live in the Boulder area," McDowell ordered. "He might have invited someone up to see his place. We have to have some idea where to start looking. His cabin could be anywhere in a seventeen-mile stretch up the canyon from Boulder to Nederland."

"I did find something interesting from the guy's supervisor," Hanks added. "He said Benny turned his truck in an hour early today. He finished his route about four o'clock."

Reece's chest tightened. Benny could be with Deanna this very minute.

"Get going on those calls," McDowell snapped. "We gotta find this guy." McDowell picked up the receiver of his own phone.

Hanks reached for the speakerphone on his desk. He called the first name on his list.

"Naw, I don't know where Caruthers lives," the man who answered the phone growled. "A real freeloader, if you know what I mean. Always around when someone has an extra beer but never offers anybody as much as a stick of gum. He's not one of the guys who stick around after work to shoot the breeze. A real weirdo, if you ask me."

"Did he ever seem . . . violent?" Hanks asked.

The man thought for a minute. "Yeah, once when the supervisor talked about changing his route. He looked ready to strangle the guy. The supervisor backed down. Yeah, I guess Caruthers could lean into someone pretty hard if he was crossed. What's the deal? Has he taken somebody out?"

Reece closed his eyes. *I pray to God he hasn't.*

The responses from the other co-workers were similar. Nobody liked Benny Caruthers. None of them had any idea where he lived. No one had ever invited him home, either. "I wouldn't trust him around my family," one fellow admitted.

When Reece thought about Deanna being in violent hands, being abused and assaulted, he felt like someone being stretched on a rack. Every minute was torture.

If only he had protected her. Heaven only knew, he'd had enough warning that some nut was after her. All that craziness with the mutilated photos. He should have zeroed in on Richard and Benny right away. Why hadn't he realized the cruel torment came from someone who had been in the neighborhood? It had taken the coal chute to make him see a truth he'd ignored earlier. And now, it was too late. The creep had Deanna. And no one knew where the bastard lived.

Officer Hanks gave the list to McDowell. "No luck."

"Everybody says the same thing," McDowell agreed. "Benny's a loner. A guy who rubs everyone the wrong way. I couldn't find a single person who gave a damn about him. And nobody had any idea where he lived. They said he drove an old Chevy to and from work."

Reece blanched. "Now we know the bastard's been stalking Deanna. That's the description Deanna gave."

"What about Public Service, Sarge? Any luck there?"

"We've got somebody en route now. Don't know how long it will take. The weather's foul out there. Roads are like ice. Nobody's going anywhere very fast."

When the phone rang a few minutes later, they all jumped. McDowell grabbed a pencil before he answered the phone.

He listened and then lowered his pencil. He swore under his breath and then barked, "Keep me posted."

"What's up?" Hanks asked.

"Damn storm. Some of the power lines are down. Ice build-up. A couple of sections of town are without electricity."

"Let me guess. The computers are out at Public Service."

"You got it. A real blackout."

"For how long?" Reece thought his chest would explode.

"A few hours at least."

The men looked at each other. A heavy silence settled on the room. No need for words. They all knew Deanna's life hung from a fragile thread—that was ready to snap at any moment.

Chapter Twenty-Three

"Don't be frightened, sweetheart," Benny soothed as Deanna tried to push him away.

"Let me go!" She writhed in his arms and pounded on his chest, but he only pressed her more tightly against him.

"Stop fighting me. I've been waiting a long time for this night, sweetheart. I want to remember every minute always. We have the whole night, but if you fight me, the party's over."

The intent of his warning was horribly clear. Unless she cooperated, he'd kill her right away. And if she did? His moist lips and leering eyes gave her the answer. Her heart raced and shivers crept up her spine. She had to play along with him. Self-preservation was her only choice. She lowered her hands.

"That's better." He nodded in approval. "That's better." His fleshy mouth spread in a broad smile.

She tried not to flinch when he touched her face. His eyes grew heavy as his exploring fingers traced her cheekbones.

"Even when you're gone, I'll close my eyes and touch your face."

Very slowly he placed his fingers on her mouth. She thought he was going to cut off her breath, but instead he caught her lips between his thumb and forefinger and squeezed. The painful pinch brought tears to her eyes.

"I'll always remember your sweet mouth," he whispered, lowering his face.

Pain and revulsion overrode Deanna's passivity. She jerked her head to one side. "No!"

He swore and imprisoned her face between his hands. He shoved his face close to hers, his breath reeking of cheap wine. "All those Christmas parties, you never kissed me under the mistletoe. Not once."

Deanna choked back a protest. *You were a repulsive brat! Obnoxious. Ellen's horrible younger brother.*

"You never gave me a valentine, did you?" he upbraided her.

"I don't remember."

"I hate you for ignoring me the way you did." He buried his face in her hair. "But I've always loved your perfume. It used to drive me crazy." He gave a jagged laugh. "Every time I sat close to you, I wanted to press up against you and smell your hair and clothes. Sometimes I'd sit down beside you, getting as close as I could. But you'd always lean away from me. You did, didn't you?''

She moistened her lips. "Yes. I'm sorry."

His eyes grew cold. "You didn't want me to touch you. But now I can be as close to you as I like. Now I *can* touch you. Just the way I fondled the sweet-smelling things in your drawers."

Deanna tried to keep her repulsion from showing. "I didn't know you went through my things."

He nodded proudly. "I handled everything. But I was careful to leave everything just as it was," he added quickly. "You never knew the dozens of times I was in your house when you were gone. Unless I wanted you to know."

"You put the teddy bear in the chair and moved the furniture, didn't you?"

He beamed, and she grasped the chance to distract him. "You had us all fooled. I never knew it was you, Benny. You were too clever." She tried to smile.

"I was, wasn't I? Watching you all the time. And you never even knew."

"No, I never guessed. Tell me what else you did." She took a deep breath and tried to control her shaky voice.

"I made copies of the keys your folks left hanging in the kitchen. There was one for the store until you changed the locks. Of course, I didn't need one to get in the house," he bragged. "I used the old coal chute."

She tried to hide the shock that his words gave her. She managed to say, "Why don't we sit down and eat while we talk? Enjoy all the delicious food. I'm hungry now. All that dancing has given me an appetite. The frosting on the cake is the best I've ever tasted. And the heart-shaped cookies are wonderful. We can't let everything go to waste, can we? Not when you've gone to so much trouble to decorate everything." She knew she was babbling, but food had always been Benny's Achilles' heel. She prayed that he would respond to the idea of eating rather than forcing his amorous intentions upon her.

"I'm glad you like everything," he said. "I did it all just for you. And I have something else to show you. Another surprise." He kept a firm hand on her shoulder as they walked back to the table.

The lights flickered, went out for a split second and then came back on again. He laughed. "I'd better light the candles. I wouldn't be surprised if the electricity went out. It does sometimes in a storm. But we don't care, do we, Foxy?"

Her stomach was in worse condition than it had been before. The sight of her plate, still loaded with cake, candy and cookies, increased her nausea. She didn't want to drink any of the wine. Her head was fuzzy enough with lack of food and with fear. He seemed to read her thoughts, because he filled up the glass he had spilled earlier and handed it to her.

"Drink up." He watched her as she put the glass to her lips and took a gulp of the vinegary liquid.

"Now have a chocolate. They go good together."

She knew he would force-feed her again if she didn't cooperate. She bit down on the gooey center of a dipped chocolate. The sugary sweetness turned her stomach, but she managed to swallow it. She quickly pressed a paper napkin to her lips, willing the wine and candy to stay down.

Benny was filling his plate again. At every child-hood party, he had stuffed cake and ice cream into his mouth as if afraid he'd never get his share. She wondered how he had managed to lose the fat he'd carried around for so many years. He must have been controlling his diet somehow. At the moment, he was acting like an alcoholic going on a binge.

The two red candles glowed brightly on the table when the electric lights flickered again. He grabbed her arm and waited. He wasn't going to take a chance that she might get away from him if the lights went out. He sat so close to her that even if she managed to scoot her chair back from the table, she couldn't be quick enough to get away.

Deanna prayed that a blackout wouldn't put a quick end to his gluttony and turn his mind to some-thing else. After a few more flickers, the electricity stayed on.

He released her arm and forced more wine on her. She feared that if she drank any more, she'd be un-able to stand on her feet.

"Drink up. A toast to sweethearts," he said, clicking his glass against hers.

She made a pretense of sipping the horrid drink.

"What else did you have to show me?" she asked, trying to cope with her whirling head, building nausea and stabbing fear. She had to stay in control of the conversation. Keep him diverted.

He grinned at her with sticky lips. "A surprise." He reached in to his back pocket and drew out a new hunting knife with red ribbons hanging from the hilt. "Just for you."

She stared at it in horror. The crimson ribbons fell across his hand like stripes of blood. He held it lovingly and flashed it in front of her eyes.

"Touch it," he ordered.

She raised a trembling hand and put a finger on the shiny blade.

"Pretty, huh? A cupid's dagger. All shiny and beautiful. I wanted something special for you."

She didn't need to ask what he was going to do with it. With sickening certainty, she knew. *He was going to plunge the dagger through her heart in the same way he had pinned the valentine to her front door.*

"Cupid's dagger will make you my sweetheart forever," he bragged, verifying his murderous intent.

She wanted to scream, plead with him, throw herself on his mercy, but his narrowed eyes stopped the words in her throat.

"Everything's ready," he assured her as if to waylay any concern she might have about his preparations. "When the party's over, I'll carry you up the hill to a small cave above the cabin. I'll bury you there. No one else will know. Just you and me, Foxy. I've got a place ready. A secret love shrine."

She drew away from the knife. He quickly circled her wrist with an iron grip. "It'll be all right. You'll see. I'll never forget you. I know you like flowers and I'll bring you some—nice fresh red roses. You'll like that, won't you?"

She turned her head, unable to look into his crazed smile. He loosened the grip he had on her wrist and stroked her arm.

"You won't be lonely. I'll come and sit by your side. There won't be anyone else around to bother us." His mouth turned down in an ugly frown. "Your lover, Reece, won't get between us anymore."

His name dispelled a rising numbness. "Reece," she echoed.

"I knew what was going on that night he stayed," he told her in an accusing tone. "He ruined everything. I wanted you to be alone that night. I let myself into your house and moved all the furniture. I was going to wake you up in the middle of the night, calling softly from Krissie's room. I had it all planned. But when I saw he was with you, I left. He's always been in the way. But no more. I have plans for Reece Ryndell. When everything's done, the only person left to love you will be me. Nobody else. Not even that kid of yours."

A surge of adrenaline raced through her like wildfire. Krissie! He had killed her parents. And now he threatened her daughter.

Deanna went wild. She shoved the table and lurched out of her chair. With a wild swing of her arms, she knocked over the two lighted candles.

A stack of party napkins went up in flames. The paper tablecloth caught fire. Instantly, the table was a blazing inferno. Benny grabbed the nearly empty bottle of wine and tried to put out the flames, but the fire had spread to the table legs. Billowing smoke followed Deanna as she bounded for the front door. Benny coughed and shouted obscenities as he dashed to the kitchen for water.

Deanna jerked open the door. Cold air rushed in to fan the flames. Outside, white snow gave a pristine brightness to the area in front of the cabin. A band of black trees stretched beyond the narrow road where the Chevy was parked, but she couldn't reach the thick evergreens without being seen against the drifted snow.

She fled around the side of the log cabin, hugging the wall. She gave a hurried glance in a side window of the front room. Benny was emptying a teakettle on the last burst of flames. The fire was nearly out. He would be after her in another minute.

Her mind raced. He'd know which direction she'd gone because of the trail she'd left in the snow. She had to get away from the house and into the nearby wooded area, where darkness would conceal her and her tracks.

She bounded away from the side of the house and into a drift of snow that stopped her flat in her tracks. She'd run into a snow-covered stack of cut logs. The force of her body hitting them dislodged the pile. The whole stack began to shift. Logs roared down the steep slope with the sound of falling bowling pins.

"Foxy?" Benny's voice sounded from the front of the house.

She just had time to retreat to the rear of the house and dart around the corner before the clatter of rolling wood brought him running to the disintegrating woodpile.

"Foxy, where are you?"

She couldn't go any farther. The rear wall of the house had been built flush with a sheer rise of mountain cliff. She was trapped.

Benny stood only a few feet away. "Foxy, come back," he yelled.

Mounds of snow-covered shrubs and a thick stand of trees at the bottom of the hill offered concealment. The wood had made paths in the snow as it tumbled downward. He must think she'd gone down the hill, her footsteps lost in the tracks made by the sliding logs.

"Foxy! I'm coming after you."

She waited until he was nearly at the bottom of the incline before she darted around the corner and raced toward the front of the house.

As luck would have it, he looked up and saw her. "There you are!"

Bitter cold sapped her breath as she fled across the clearing in front of the cabin. The narrow road was barely visible. The old Chevy was parked heading downward. She jerked open the front door, praying that he might have left the keys in it.

He hadn't.

She was about to leap from the car again, but in the last split second she changed her mind. She slammed the door shut and locked it. On older model cars, the transmission didn't lock when the key was removed. With a hope born of desperation, she released the emergency brake. If she could get the car rolling, she might be able to keep going down the narrow road until it connected with the main highway. Frantically, she turned the steering wheel back and forth.

"Foxy!" Benny came up over the top of the hill and started running toward the car. His strong legs were plowing through the snow that covered the clearing in front of the house when the car began to slide forward.

Deanna hunched over the steering wheel as the Chevy quickly gathered momentum. The runaway car sped by the trees and boulders looming up on both sides. Deanna peered through a snow-speckled windshield, her vision limited by the lack of head-lights and the unfamiliar road. She prayed that the car would keep rolling until it reached the bottom of the hill.

When she saw a flicker of light not far below, she knew she had a chance of making it!

Her sense of victory was short-lived. A moment later, something dark rose up in front of the car. A cliff? A bank?

A crunch of metal and glass exploded in her ears. She screamed and then fell silent as her forehead struck the hard rim of the steering wheel.

Chapter Twenty-Four

A thousand jagged pieces of pain shot through her head. Terror coated her body in hot sweat. She fought the hands that pulled her arms down to her sides. *He was going to tie her up again.* His leering face rose behind her closed lids. She had to get away. She raised her hands and tried to remove the tight band that encircled her skull.

Tears flowed down her cheeks. Her heavy eyelids lifted. She flinched as a hand touched her cheek.

"It's all right, love."

She frowned and raised her hand to her head again.

"Leave the bandage alone, Dee Dee."

Light from a window touched the face of the man leaning over her. A feeble smile touched her lips. She was disoriented and confused, but the relief that sped through her needed no explanation. Reece was with her. She was safe . . . safe . . . safe.

She slept then, and when she awakened the next time, the window was dark, but soft lights illuminated the restful room.

Reece's lanky frame filled a nearby chair. As he slept, his long legs were stretched out in front of him and his arms were folded across his chest. For a long time, she just stared at his beloved face. She wanted to etch every line and plane in her memory. A wonderment at the deep love she had always had for him spilled through her.

She frowned. How had she gotten here? Fragmented thoughts floated to the surface. The cabin. The fire. Guiding the runaway car down the mountain road. Everything else was murky.

As if Reece sensed her intense scrutiny, he opened his eyes. Relief instantly crossed his face. He sat down on the edge of her bed and squeezed her hand. "How are you feeling, sleepyhead?"

"Confused."

"What else is new?" he teased. His eyes were a soft, caressing blue. He touched a light kiss to her mouth. "You're in Boulder Community Hospital. An ambulance brought you here after you banged your head on the steering wheel."

"How long have I been here?"

"About thirty hours."

Panic rushed through her. "Krissie! I've got to get home to Krissie."

He gently held her on the pillow. "No, you don't. Krissie's fine. Just fine." He stroked her hair. "She's in good hands. Has all kinds of people spoiling her.

You're the one that needs taking care of. And I intend to see that you get plenty of rest while that bump on your head heals."

She frowned. "Everything's kind of fuzzy," she admitted. "I remember getting into the car. Trying to glide it down the road . . . to the highway. I almost made it. Then I crashed into something." She was puzzled. "A tree? A rock?"

"A police car."

Her eyes widened. "A police car?"

He grinned at her horrified expression. "It's true. Sergeant McDowell managed to get Benny's address from a butane gas company. He alerted a patrol car in the area. Two policemen were driving up the road, and all of a sudden an old Chevy comes at them out of the dark with you at the wheel. Fortunately, neither of the officers were hurt and you got out of it with a minor concussion."

As the veil on her memory began lifting, she told him about the horrors of her abduction. As Reece listened, fury blazed in his eyes. He swore under his breath and then he told her what had happened after Nellie found the store closed up.

"How did you know to look for Benny?"

He explained that Nicki's remark about Ellen's bratty little boys had triggered his memory about the way Richard and Benny had behaved when they were children. "I was sure it was Richard until I learned that he's in prison. And now his little brother, Benny, is going to join him," he said with grim satisfaction.

Deanna shivered, remembering Benny's cupid's dagger and what he'd said and done. She told Reece that Benny had admitted that he'd killed her parents.

"The guy's a real psychopath. He went berserk when the police took him in. Thank God, you got away from him." He lifted her hand and pressed it to his lips. Then he said, "I have something for you. This place isn't exactly where I'd pictured giving it to you when I bought it, but being able to slip it around your lovely neck means more to me than ever." He handed her the gift.

"It's beautiful," she whispered. A small gold and amethyst heart dangled from a fragile chain. "Put it on me."

He took it from her trembling hand and fastened it around her neck. She held the jeweled heart in her hand. A symbol of love. A promise of warmth and caring. A new life beginning. "Thank you."

She knew now how Reece had felt when he thought he was going to die without telling her how much he cared about her. She had felt the same way during all those hours that she'd lain helpless, expecting her life to end at any moment. Her eyes grew misty. "I've been in love with you all my life, Reece Ryndell. I never want to be away from you again."

A small smile tugged at the corner of his lips. "Is this a good time to ask you to marry me?"

She slipped her arms around his neck. "The best."

My Valentine 1994

Celebrate the most romantic day of the year with
MY VALENTINE 1994
a collection of original stories, written by
four of Harlequin's most popular authors...

MARGOT DALTON
MURIEL JENSEN
MARISA CARROLL
KAREN YOUNG

Available in February, wherever
Harlequin Books are sold.

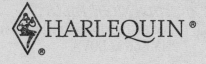

HARLEQUIN ®

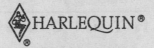